ST LUCIA MYSTERY

BERNICE BLOOM

DEAR READERS

Thank you so much for buying the magnificent story of Mary & Ted's adventure in St Lucia. I really hope you enjoy it.

The story features a woman named Cara Jeffries who heads off to St Lucia for three months and gets herself into considerable trouble. A month later, when Mary and Ted go to the island on their honeymoon, they stumble into Cara's story after finding a purse on the beach.

What should Mary do? Should she relax and enjoy her honeymoon and hope the girl is found? Or should she launch herself headlong into the middle of the operation to find her, risking her life, and Ted's, as they come face-to-face with armed gangs and dodgy officials?

What do you think they do?

The dynamic duo get stuck in. Though they are not the greatest gift to undercover policing, their hearts are in the right place as they investigate.

Moving back between Cara's story and Mary's story, this book takes you on a wonderful journey on a beautiful Caribbean Island.

DEAR READERS

I hope you enjoy it! And thanks again for your support. It is greatly appreciated. To everyone who has bought a book, left me a lovely review or just commented on the Facebook page – thank you from the bottom of my heart.

Now, let's go over to Cara and Mary to guide you through the story...

Bernice Bloom
Hampton Court, 2024

CHAPTER ONE

Cara's story: 1ˢᵗ June

IT WAS one of those lovely shimmering, sunlit days. Cara slipped on her sunglasses and sat back in her seat, thinking about the long summer ahead.

'Are you OK?' asked Jools.

'I'm fine.'

'You know you're going to have the time of your life, don't you?'

Cara offered a half-smile and looked in the mirror at her other two friends, jigging along to the music in the back seat.

She knew how lucky she was that her three best friends were coming with her to the airport.

The four of them were packed tightly into a small car juddering along the M4 with music and cigarette smoke curling out of the window into the gentle, early summer air.

'I feel like we're in a movie, driving through LA...this is glorious,' said Rachel, leaning out of the window and taking a large drag of her cigarette, breathing out and watching the smoke vanish into the air, a fleeting mist leaving the merest trace of its presence behind.

'Except in the movie, we'd be in one of those enormous Cadillacs, not this little mini.'

'Oy, don't diss my motor,' said Jools, stroking the steering wheel affectionately as the old car limped towards the airport building.

'Just drop me here,' said Cara, yelling over the sound of Taylor Swift. 'I'll be fine from here.'

'Nope,' said Jools, as she swung the car towards the short-stay carpark. 'We're coming with you right up until the moment you get onto the plane.'

'We might even get on the plane with you and help you with your seat belt,' said Katherine. 'We're not dumping you on the pavement and leaving you to fend for yourself.'

'I'm thinking of coming with you,' said Rachel. 'I'm in the mood for a night flight and a Caribbean adventure.'

'I wish you were all coming. I'm going to miss you guys so much,' said Cara. 'I'm starting to wonder what on earth I'm doing, heading off to the other side of the world on my own.'

Jools found a parking space and braked abruptly.

'What you're doing, my love is going to have the time of your life. You'll be refreshed and tanned when you get back and have put that rat, Dean, out of your mind.

The mere mention of Dean and Cara felt the pain in her chest sharpen and twinge before fading again.

'It's just that...'
'What?'
'I don't know. I've never done anything like this before.'

'Nope, but there's a first time for everything,' said Katherine. 'You are going to have the time of your life.'

'Come on. Let's talk about this on the way in. Perhaps we can get a coffee somewhere before you go through.'

The four friends clambered out of Jools' car and helped Cara carry her luggage to the lift and down into the departure hall.

'You go and check your bags in; we'll find coffee,' said Jools.

As soon as Cara was out of sight, the women turned to one another.

'This trip will do her the world of good,' said Jools. 'I hope it all goes OK. I do worry about her. She's so vulnerable at the moment.'

'That's exactly why she needs to go. Anything that gets her away from Dean is all good,' said Katherine, returning to the table with coffee.

'Hopefully, she'll meet some good friends out there.'

'She's bound to,' said Rachel. 'And her nerves will go in no time. She'll sleep all the way there and wake up to sunshine and tropical sounds.'

'All done,' said Cara, returning to the women and gratefully taking the cappuccino they offered. 'I can't back out now.'

'And nor should you. We've just been talking about what a perfect trip this is for you. You'll remember it for the rest of your life.'

Cara nodded. They weren't wrong. She was studying for a master's degree when she got back, and one key component of the literature course was the study of Caribbean writers, particularly Derek Walcott, a writer from St Lucia whom she adored. His words had been particularly poignant recently as she'd coped with heartache and disappointment. She couldn't wait to find out more about him.

'I should go,' said Cara, standing up and picking up her bag. 'I'm going to miss you all.'

'We'll all be here, in the same little house when you get back,' said Rachel. 'Just get out there, have loads of fun and send us tonnes of pictures.'

Cara embraced her friends warmly and walked towards the departure gate.

'St Lucia, here I come!' she shouted, her voice a curious mix of joy and fear.

'Have the best time,' they shouted back. 'Make sure you get to know all the delicious watersports instructors.'

She smiled as she pictured the island, the tropical paradise, the escape from reality. She was about to leave everything behind for the summer, and it felt exciting, liberating, and mind-numbingly terrifying.

'Look after yourself,' shouted Katherine as Cara moved almost out of sight.

'I will, I swear,' she said, turning around for a final glance. Cara saw their faces, full of affection. They were her lifeline, her anchor, her home. She would miss them enormously, but an exciting future lay ahead.

She joined the queue to pass through security and fiddled with her passport. In the weeks and months to come, she would think back to those innocent moments as she waited at the airport and would wish, with all her might, that she had just turned around then and never got on the plane.

CHAPTER
TWO

Cara's story: 2nd June

CARA SETTLED into her seat and leaned back, closing her eyes against the hustle and bustle of noisy boarders. She'd wondered, so many times, whether this was a good idea. But there weren't many occasions on which one found oneself with a few months free & the sudden arrival of enough money to afford to go off to live on a Caribbean island for the summer. She'd have been mad not to make the trip.

'Hi,' came a voice from beside her.

'Oh, hello,' said Cara, smiling warmly at a man who began shuffling his coat and bag under the seat next to hers and dropping into it with a huge sigh.

'I didn't think I was going to make it.'

Another man standing in the aisle, putting cases into the overhead locker, sat beside him. He was very good-looking, quite tall, muscular, and extraordinarily well-dressed. She pushed a toiletry bag into the seat pocket infront of him.

'I'm Scott,' he said.

'I'm Cara.'

The man beside her introduced himself as Robbie, and they sat there in a rather uncomfortable silence: strangers, knowing they were about to spend the next 10 hours practically touching as they flew through the air.

'Are you going on holiday?' asked Robbie.

'Yes. Although, to be honest, it's a mixture of work and play.'

The awkward silence fell again until the stewardess gave her short safety talk, and the plane rumbled along the runway. Once airborne, Scott stood up and retrieved what looked like a laptop from the locker.

She noticed again how incredibly well-dressed he was, in a cream linen suit, a white shirt and soft camel-coloured loafers. His hands were immaculate, with fingernails manicured and buffed to a shine. She tucked her fingernails into the palms of her hands. She wasn't big into personal grooming. Her morning regime consisted of little more than a splash of water and a dab of Nivea. She was a windsurfer from a small village in Cornwall. No one was worried about that sort of thing in her world. From Cornwall, she'd headed to Birmingham University and no one expected students to be well-dressed. She realised that she was staring at the well-dressed man. He didn't look as if he had any place travelling in economy. He didn't look as if he had any place in this decade.

'I'm sorry, did you say something?' she asked.

'I just asked whether you were travelling alone.'

'I am.'

'And what's this 'mixture of work and play' you're off to do, then?'

'I'm teaching watersports at a lovely hotel in St Lucia for the summer.'

'That sounds fun,' said Robbie, suddenly very interested. 'Are you a qualified teacher? You should teach me; I'd love to learn.'

'I'd be very happy to,' she said.

'Is that what you do in England? Teach watersports?'

'No, I've just finished my degree, and I'm doing a master's degree when I return.'

It was Scott's turn to be impressed. 'How wonderful,' he said. 'What subject?'

'English,' she replied. 'The master's course has a module on Caribbean writers.'

'I don't think I know any Caribbean writers.'

'There's a writer called Derek Walcott who I'm obsessed with,' she said. 'He's brilliant… 'A white head dipping in a rocker while the black town walked barefoot.' His writing is warm, sensitive and meaningful.'

'Gosh, that's a lovely quote. I've never heard of him.'

'You have to look him up when you get to St Lucia. I'm determined to find out all about him while I'm there.'

'I'd love to come with you,' said Scott. 'We must exchange numbers. I'm unsure how interested Robbie will be, but I'd love to learn more.'

Robbie was sitting back, headphones on, drumming his fingers on the armrest, oblivious to their conversation.

'Of course,' she said. 'I'd like that.'

Cara felt very pleased with herself. They'd only just taken off, and she'd made a friend already. It would be great to have someone to come with her to find out more about the great writer. She snuggled back into her seat and closed her eyes, thinking about the trip ahead, before slowly fading into sleep before the plane had even left the tarmac..

∼

As soon as Cara emerged from the airport building, she felt the heat rising to greet her. It was beautiful. She felt warm and excited. She was here, on a beautiful Caribbean island, with three glorious months ahead of her. She'd been reassured by the ease with which she'd made friends on the plane and felt great confidence in the future.

'Just call us if you need anything,' Robbie and Scott had said, with Scott reiterating how much he'd love to join Cara on trips to landmarks around St Lucia, which celebrated the life of Walcott.

She looked up and down the road for the car that was due to collect her and take her to Hotel Hibiscus. She'd received a text saying a pickup truck with the registration number PA1988 would be there, but she couldn't see anything. She put her bags down and prepared to reply to the text when a pickup truck raced around the corner and pulled up alongside her.

'Cara?' said a man with the widest smile she'd ever seen.

'Yes.'

The man jumped out of the truck, grabbed her bags and threw them into the back before inviting her to climb in. 'I'm Happy,' he said. 'Welcome to St Lucia.'

Inside the truck was a man called Chuckles. Cara smiled at the joy of their names as she looked over at them, both grinning in the sunlight, dressed in fabulously brightly coloured shirts and looking as if they had not a care in the world.

'What do you know about Amizan?'

'Sorry?'

'Amizan - do you know much about it?'

'Sorry, I don't know what that is.'

'Amizan is the name of the watersports company you work for.'

Chuckles glanced at Happy; she could tell they thought she must be nuts.

'Oh, sorry - I didn't know it was called that. I thought it was Hotel Hibiscus.'

'Well, yes, we are based next to Hotel Hibiscus, and we run all the watersports for guests at the hotel, but the watersports club is called Amizan - that's Creole for 'fun'.'

'Sorry, I should probably know where I'm working.'

'Hey, not a problem. Peace and love. We are a happy bunch of people. There are 12 of us working there, and summer is our busy time. You will have great fun.'

'Thank you. I hope so,' she said.

'If you have any questions at all, just ask us.'

'Tell me a little about the place I'll be staying. Where is Lobster Bay?'

'It's in the island's northwest, not far from Rodney Bay. Have you heard of that? Lobster Bay is wonderful, and so is Rodney. It's a very beautiful place. The island is small, so it is easy to travel around and see the whole place.'

'Are we near to Castries, the capital?'

'Yes, we are. That is also in the northwest, but a bit further down the island. I can take you there any time you want to go.'

∽

The pickup truck swept into the hotel grounds...along the glamorous driveway, stopping in front of an incredible colonial-style building with beautiful flowers, trees, and a luscious green lawn.

'Wow!'

'I know,' said Happy. 'It's beautiful, isn't it?'

'I don't think I've ever seen anywhere more beautiful.' Cara scanned the gardens, which stretched out as far as she could see. Butterflies gathered inside her. This was exciting. Imagine living here for three months? She had struck gold.

'We're just around the back here,' he said, crunching the gears on the pickup truck as he continued his journey around Hotel Hibiscus and down to Lobster Bay. The lovely gardens ran straight down to a private beach. Happy pulled over into a small carpark and pointed out the water sports hut. It looked like a ski chalet. To the side of it were lots of small huts.

'See those,' said Happy, pointing to them. 'That's where the staff live. Two people in each hut, so it's a bit of a squeeze, but you are the only female here at the moment, so you get one to yourself.'

The huts looked perfectly OK, just small. Certainly not as glamorous as the hotel where she thought she was staying.

'Let's get your suitcases out, and I'll give you time to settle in. Come over to Amizan when you're ready.'

'Sure,' said Cara, taking the key from Happy and letting herself in.

There were bunk beds, a small bathroom with a stale, unpleasant aroma and a tatty wardrobe that looked like it had been through two world wars. The walls were painted a miserable, bruised avocado, making them dark and dismal. She vowed to buy some lovely yellow paint to cheer it up. She'd even paint the wardrobe and buy a cream rug and lamp. With some flowers and plants, it would look really good. She switched on the lights and noticed there was no shade. She'd buy one of those as well. She wanted a home from home and would create one on the edge of the Caribbean Sea.

CHAPTER
THREE

Cara's story: 2nd June

THE SUN HUNG low in the sky as Cara ambled back to her accommodation, her mind filled with the day's experiences. The watersports centre had been her first stop, where she'd encountered her new colleagues. Their laughter had reached her ears long before seeing them, their voices carrying on the salty breeze.

As she approached, they were engrossed in a boisterous game, their sun-kissed bodies colliding in a tangle of limbs. Golden hair, bleached by countless hours under the sun, glinted in the light, while vibrant board shorts added splashes of colour to the scene. The air was filled with an infectious camaraderie, the kind often found among those who spend their days riding the waves.

Cara had noted the absence of any women, realising she was the sole female in this laid-back brotherhood..

Now, as she settled into a deck chair, the weathered wood creaking beneath her weight, Cara let out a contented sigh. The last rays of the day caressed her skin, the warmth a soothing balm after the eventful day. She knew that navigating this male-dominated world would have its challenges, but for now, she was content to bask in the tranquillity of the moment, her eyes drifting shut as the sun descended towards the horizon.

The waves lapped against the shore, providing such a soothing soundtrack that she felt no need for headphones or her book. She lost herself in the moment instead. How rarely she did that…abandoning all stimuli to the present moment. It was absolute bliss.

But, even in this paradise, the ache in her heart persisted. Unbidden and unwelcome thoughts of Dean crept into her mind, closing down the lovely peacefulness and filling her head with painful images.

She tried again to focus on the sun's warmth on her skin and the gentle caress of the breeze. But the memories were relentless, each one a sharp reminder of the love she had lost. The future she had once envisioned, filled with laughter, shared adventures, and the promise of forever, now shattered at her feet.

Cara's fingers dug into the armrests of the deckchair, anchoring herself to the present. She willed herself to breathe, to find solace in the natural wonders around her.

∼

'Hey, beautiful, can I help you?'

Cara looked up to see a handsome man in a pink and purple floral shirt. The men liked their colours here. British men could learn a lot.

'I saw you walking around, and I thought I'd come and introduce myself. My name's Tajo.'

'Oh, hi. I'm Cara.'

'Do you mind if I join you?'

Before waiting for an answer, he dropped onto the grass beside her and stretched his long legs before him. They were as glossy as conkers, like they'd been polished to a shine. He saw her looking, and Cara felt herself blush.

'Are you working in the water sports department?' he asked.

'I am, yes.'

'Have you done sailing and windsurfing and all the things before?'

'Yes, all my life. I was born by the seaside; even when tiny, we were down on the beach whenever possible.'

'Watersports are your passion?'

'Yes, I suppose they are, really.'

'It's good to have a passion,' he said, nodding as if he'd said something incredibly wise.

'You are English,' he said, as if he were revealing something to her that she did not already know. He was looking at her with an intensity that made her feel nervous. 'Why are you here?'

'I thought this would be a great way to spend the summer.'

'Good decision. This is a perfect way to spend the summer.'

They smiled at one another.

'What do you do?' she asked.

'Investments and banking,' he said. 'Making people's money grow, grow, grow. I am the money tree.'

'That's interesting.'

'No, I know what you're thinking - it sounds boring. It's

not, though. I meet people from all over the island and help them to make the most of their money. This is the rich part of the island, where holidaymakers go. I can help them. My passion is helping poor people who are struggling to pay bills. If I can help them, I feel I am contributing to the world.'

'To be fair, that does sound amazing,' said Cara.

'Life is for living,' he replied. He had a habit of saying these odd statements that might sound crass and inauthentic if spoken in an English tongue but somehow sounded worldly-wise from him.

'I am also an investor in the hotel,' he revealed, his voice low and measured.

'Oh wow. That's impressive.'

He waved his hand dismissively, a gentle smile playing on his lips. 'No, not at all. Not remotely so. I made a lot of money from investing wisely and chose to invest in this hotel. It's very straightforward.'

As he spoke, Cara leaned in, drawn to his confidence and humility. A comfortable silence settled between them, the only sound being the sea and the gentle rustling of the leaves in the warm breeze. Cara smiled and settled back in her deckchair once more.

'What are you reading?' he asked, spotting her book tucked into the side of her chair.

'Oh, it's a biography of Derek Walcott.'

Again, he said nothing. He stared at her with enormous brown eyes as if she were the only woman in the world.

'I love his poetry.'

'Me too,' said Cara. 'I will take you to the museum devoted to his work. It's in Castries. You will love it there.'

'Oh, that would be great,' she said.

'I will take you anywhere you would like to go.'

Cara opened the book's cover to reveal a list of places she'd read about in Walcott's work and was keen to visit for herself.

'You and I will go to all these places. I will introduce you to the real St Lucia, and you will fall in love with it.'

'Thank you,' she said, smiling at him.

'Are you free tomorrow? I will take you.'

'I start the new job tomorrow.'

'After work?'

'Sure. I finish at 2.30pm. Shall we say 3pm?'

CHAPTER

FOUR

3rd June

Cara stepped into the water sports centre, her heart pounding with a mixture of excitement and apprehension. In the room were the men she'd met yesterday when she'd popped in to introduce herself. She noticed their gazes scrutinising her every move. She could sense their doubts, their unspoken questions about her abilities.

Determined to prove herself, Cara grabbed her gear and headed out to the beach. Her first client, a middle-aged man eager to learn windsurfing, awaited her instruction. Cara guided him through the basics, precisely demonstrating each technique. As the lesson progressed, the man's confidence grew, and soon he was gliding across the water with ease.

Her co-workers watched from the shore in amazement, their scepticism slowly fading. As she returned to the centre, the once-doubtful faces now held a newfound respect.

'Come and join us for lunch,' said Tom, by far the friendliest of the men.

'I'd love to,' she said.

They walked from the seafront to a small café, lodged in a cove, out of sight.

'Wow, this looks nice,' she said, clambering onto one of the tall bar stools and taking the menu offered by the waiter.

She ordered a vegetable roti with salad. The guys ordered burgers and fries.

'Right. I need to know all about you. Who's first?'

'I'm Tom, and I like water sports. These are my friends, Pete and Andy.'

'Very nice to meet you,' she said. 'What do you do when you're not hanging around on Caribbean islands?'

'Nothing. Just at uni, to be honest.'

'What did you study?'

'Veterinary studies at Bristol.'

'Bloody hell. That's incredible. Hardly 'nothing'. So why are you out here instead of helping injured pets?'

'It's a gap year type thing. I finished the degree and thought I fancied a break. I did some travelling around South America and ended up backpacking in Cuba. I met some guys who knew of this place. I headed down here, and the rest is history. Your turn, Pete.'

'Same sort of thing,' said Pete, momentarily pausing when the food arrived. 'I did environmental science at Manchester Uni, then worked at a conservation charity for a year. I had a friend who used to work here. He knew they were looking to recruit, and I thought it sounded like fun, so I hopped on a plane. Over to you, Andy.'

'I didn't go to uni. I went to art college and studied graphic design. I couldn't face a traditional 9-to-5 so I became a freelance photographer. I came out here to work, thinking it would be the perfect chance to build my photography portfolio while enjoying a laid-back island lifestyle.'

'Have you taken lots of pictures while you've been here?'

The other two sniggered as she asked.

'What's the matter? Why are you laughing.'

'He was taking pictures of you out on the water this morning.'

'Was he? Let me see.'

'Tom made me delete them. He said it wasn't very respectful. Sorry if you think that too.'

Cara felt a rush of affection towards Tom. When she looked at him, he was blushing.

∼

Tajo proved to be true to his word. At 3pm precisely, he knocked on the door to Cara's hut.

'A trip to Walcott land?' he said, leading her to his car parked outside the hotel grounds. 'Our first stop is Castries. The capital of this fine island.'

Castries was busy, much more bustling than Lobster Bay where their hotel and water sports club operated in splendid isolation. Cara felt quite alarmed by the pace of city life. She had been much more at home in their oceanfront home.

'Down here,' said Tajo, negotiating the busy roads expertly. It was great to be shown around the place by a local; Tajo knew where to park and the shortcuts he needed to take to get us to our destination as quickly as possible.

'Let's go,' he said after parking the car on a small side street just outside the town centre.

'Now then, I've been doing some research. Derek Walcott was born right here in this village. This is where it all started.'

Cara listened intently, absorbing every word. She could almost picture a young Walcott running through these streets, his mind already brimming with the verses that would one day earn him a Nobel Prize.

They soon arrived at a modest wooden house. 'Here we are,' Tajo announced, his voice hushed with reverence. 'This is where Walcott spent his formative years, where his love for language and storytelling first began.'

Cara stood before the house, her eyes taking in every detail. The wooden shutters, the faded paint, and the small porch.

Tajo led her inside. The interior was simple yet charming, filled with remnants of a life well-lived. Photographs adorned the walls, capturing moments from Walcott's past. Books of poetry, their spines well-worn, lined the shelves.

'Can you imagine the conversations that must have taken place here?' Tajo mused, his fingers tracing the edge of a faded photograph.

Cara closed her eyes, letting her imagination transport her back in time. She could almost hear the clinking of cups, the aroma of freshly brewed tea filling the air. She pictured Walcott hunched over a desk, his pen scratching against paper as he poured his heart onto the page.

As they explored the house, Tajo shared anecdotes and insights that he'd obviously learned through a guidebook. She was incredibly flattered that he'd gone to all this trouble.

'Shall we go and see his writing room?'

'Oh yes, I'd love that.'

Walcott's writing room was a sanctuary, a space where he could retreat into solitude and focus on his craft. Located on the house's second floor, it overlooked the gardens.

Inside, the writing room was sparsely furnished. A large wooden desk occupied the centre of the room, strewn with papers, notebooks, and writing implements. Bookshelves lined the walls, filled with volumes of poetry, literature, and reference materials that served as sources of inspiration and knowledge.

The writing room's windows were adorned with billowing curtains that filtered the tropical sunlight, casting a warm and inviting glow over the space.

A comfortable armchair nestled in one corner of the room, while a small side table held a collection of his favourite books and manuscripts. The room was a sanctuary of creativity.

'In this intimate space, surrounded by the sights, sounds, and scents of his beloved St. Lucia, Derek Walcott crafted some of his most celebrated works, leaving behind a literary legacy that continues to inspire and resonate with audiences worldwide,' said Tajo.

'Thank you, my personal guidebook,' said Cara.

'This afternoon, we'll head to Marigot Bay,' Tajo announced, his smile widening. 'It's an inlet that Walcott wrote about in his poetry. It's like stepping into a painting. I have some friends who live there. They have a yacht. If they're out today, we'll go and visit them. We'll get a small boat over there.'

'Oh wow. This is amazing. But you have to let me pay for the boat ride. You bought the tickets to go round Walcott's house. It's not fair for you to pay for everything.'

'Just relax,' he said. 'Sit back and enjoy yourself.'

The gentle breeze caressed her face as the boat sped across the water. Tajo's soft and melodic voice filled the air as he recited verses from Walcott's poetry. The man had really done his homework.

After a walk around, with Tajo valiantly pointing out a range of landmarks and offering fascinating facts about Walcott's life, they decided to stop for dinner.

'I know just the place to go,' said Tajo. He took her to a breathtakingly romantic restaurant on a ridge with a gorgeous view of the bay stretching below them. It felt like they were dining in the clouds. Cara had fresh-caught mahi-mahi in a creamy callaloo sauce followed by a decadent chocolate lava cake, savouring each bite as the sun began to set.

CHAPTER

FIVE

Mary's story: 4th July

'OH MY GOD. Look chickens. There are chickens everywhere - scampering around the place without a care in the world. Ted, have you seen the chickens?'

'Yes, love. You can't miss the chickens.'

'They are everywhere!'

'Indeed they are.' Ted nods, clearly unimpressed with my chicken chat.

'Now look. Up ahead,' I cry, clapping my hands with delight and jumping up and down like a four-year-old. Ahead of me, there are more chickens than you've ever seen in your life; seriously, they are everywhere, all clucking as they waddle down the track towards me. I swear to God, if these feathery little creatures find themselves a courageous and visionary leader and rise in defiance, they'll take over the world.

'Ladies and gentlemen, welcome to the beautiful island of St Lucia, the jewel of the Caribbean Ocean,' says a lady in a gentle, languid voice. 'I am Sambina. If you're staying at Lobster Bay, please gather over here.' She's smartly dressed and holding a clipboard, so Ted and I do exactly as she says. It's a brave person who ignores instructions imparted by a smartly dressed woman clutching a clipboard. 'Please wait for one moment, and we'll soon have you on your way,' she says.

'I hope so. I'm dying to get to the hotel. I'm bloody starving,' says Ted.

'I can help there,' I say, pulling a large egg mayonnaise roll from my bag. Ted's eyes almost pop out of his head. I feel like a magician. He couldn't look more surprised if I pulled a white rabbit out of it or released a flight of doves. I purchased the roll before getting on the plane and managed not to consume it during the flight. Ted takes it eagerly and peels back the cling film. An unpleasant, pungent, sour, rotten odour is released.

'Don't show the chickens,' I say. 'They might be related to the sandwich.' Ted shakes his head and raises his hand as if to warn me that he wants no more chicken talk. He then takes a giant bite of the roll.

Egg mayonnaise is gathered in a clump on his chin and smeared around his mouth. He looks like a five-year-old.

'Only four of you heading to Lobster Bay today,' says Sambina. 'You must be Mary and Ted. Meet Isabella and Barney.'

The couple we're introduced to are incredibly well-dressed. The woman, in particular, looks like she's dressed to go to the opera in Milan. The high heels, elegant pencil skirt and expensive jewellery look as if they have been chosen with little regard for the steaming temperatures.

She says 'good morning' in divinely accented English, and I feel like curtseying. How can anyone look that great when they have just come off a long-haul flight? I smile at the glamorous couple and extend my hand.

'Lovely to meet you,' I say. Ted attempts to speak but ends up spitting chewed-up eggs all over them. They both pretend not to notice as a clump of egg rolls down her sunglasses and attaches itself to the end of her nose. 'Come on, let's get to the hotel,' she says, brushing egg from her silk blouse.

We climb onto the plush minibus with powerful air conditioning and a bottle of water on each seat. 'This is lovely, isn't it?' I say to our travelling companions. Isabella smiles rather patronisingly while Barney ignores me completely. Ted finishes his snack by scooping out the egg mayonnaise in the cling film. He's about to start licking the packaging until I glare at him. We're simply not in the right company for this sort of behaviour.

'Have you been to St Lucia before?' I ask Isabella.

'Many times.'

'Is it as lovely as it seems? I've never been before. I can't wait.'

'It is indeed. Very beautiful.' '

Are there lots of places to explore?'

'We're not explorers. I like to relax on holiday. We have very stressful lives. We'll be lying by the pool, won't we, darling.'

'I'm not sure about that,' replies Barney with more than an element of frustration. 'I like to think we'll see some of the island while we're here.'

'My husband is very senior in the police force,' says Isabella, smiling at me with inflated lips. Her head is tilted like a puppy watching a fly.

'Very good,' I say. What else can I say? Barney's not listening. He's switched his phone on and is catching up on emails and texts or something.

Isabella shakes her head, folds her arms, and sits back in her seat as if this is all simply too much for her. She looks like Grace Kelly in those lovely old movies. Her husband is no slouch either; he has more than a touch of the George Clooney about him. I look at Ted in his scruffy old T-shirt and crumpled shorts with an egg on them.

'What's the matter?' he asks. Bits of mayonnaise nestle in his stubble.

'Wipe your face,' I whisper.

'I'm saving it for later,' he says with a smile.

'Please, Ted. This isn't the place for our usual nonsense. We have to pretend to be sophisticated.'

'No, we don't. We'll be our usual crazy selves. Sod Miss Prim and Proper and her dull-as-ditch water husband.'

'But he's very senior in the police,' I say, mocking Isabelle's accent.

'That's more like it. Come here,' he says, pulling me in for a giant egg-flavoured kiss.

The minibus winds its way through the streets towards our hotel. As we drive along, there are more chickens on the dirt tracks (I don't comment) and banana plantations lining the road. Seeing people picking bananas, mangoes, and pineapples is thrilling but so strange. I wonder whether St Lucians are as thrilled to see people in England picking blackberries on a frosty Autumn day. I suspect not, but this is St Lucia, and it is alive with colours, smells, and unusual sights. We skirt around the edge of the tropical forests and see birds in jewel-coloured jackets lifting into the warm summer skies, guided by beams of golden sunlight filtering through the trees. I put my face up to the small open window and breathe in citrusy orange smells. It's magnificent.

Sambina stands up at the front of the coach and welcomes us again to 'this island paradise.'

'Any questions?' she asks.

'Yes, I do,' says Isabella. 'I heard that it's very dangerous here. Is that true?'

'No, it is not true. This beautiful part of St Lucia is without problems. If you are worried about anything, please talk to the personal butler assigned to your room. He will happily accompany you if you are worried.'

'It's fine. Please - there's no need for a security detail. No one feels unsafe here,' says Barney, shaking his head at his wife.

She whispers to him, and he raises his hand to stop her. But she will not be stopped.

'I'm sorry to go on about this, but my husband's in the police, and he heard that a young guest had gone missing here. Is that true?'

I gasp at this news, my gasp coming out so loud that I make myself jump. Ted looks at me as if I've lost my mind.

'That's what I've heard,' says Isabella.

'No guests have gone missing. No guest has ever gone missing. This is a safe and beautiful place and we will do everything to ensure you have a wonderful holiday.'

I glance at Ted, and he gives me the biggest smile in the world.

'Now we arrive,' says Sambina. 'Here we are, and we meet other new residents on the beach today, and you will have a lovely time.'

We clamber off the bus and are handed small white hand towels to mop our brows, a beautiful flower and some white flip-flops to wear on the beach. Ted and I slip them on while Isabella complains that she's not wearing them and insists on sticking with her designer footwear. 'Here,' says Sambina, guiding us onto the sand, where we join a group of five or six people.

We can hear Barney behind us, tutting at his wife's attempts to navigate the sand in high heels. Just as they are about to reach us, we hear loud clapping and drumming as a group of dancers come running along the beach towards us, slapping their hands on their thighs, singing and shouting.

'Welcome, welcome,' booms a man dancing among them. He wears billowing pink and yellow Bermuda shorts. As the singing stops and the drummers relax, he moves so he stands before us, in the middle of the soft white sand next to the luxurious turquoise water, arms outstretched and a smile extending the width of his face.

'You are very welcome to our beautiful sunshine island. My name is Happy, and I am glad to meet you,' he says.

I have to stop myself from jumping up and down with excitement. 'You have the best name in the world,' I shout. 'If I weren't married to Ted, I'd marry you immediately and become Mrs Happy.'

'You are very kind and beautiful,' Happy says. 'Now, if I can help you during your stay, just call out 'Happy!' from wherever you are, and I will be there. For now, I welcome you to St Lucia, the most beautiful island in the world.'

'Oh my God...' I say, gripping hold of Ted. 'It's like paradise, isn't it? This beach looks like it has been beamed down from heaven.'

Ted hugs me close to him. 'Happy honeymoon, my love,' he says. 'Let's have the best week of our lives.'

'This is going to be the holiday of a lifetime,' I agree.

Happy smiles as he watches us fondly, like a proud

father looking adoringly at his young children. His facial muscles must ache by the end of the day; the amount of smiling he does is crazy. He urges us all to look around, take in the wonder of the place, and enjoy every minute of our vacation.

'Now, you will be led to your rooms. They are all lovely chalets - very independent, but still part of the main hotel.'

I don't know what he means by that, but it doesn't matter. Nothing matters except the sight of the sky and the sea, the beautiful, unfamiliar smells, and the wonder of what the week will bring.

A group of men in white uniforms appear and spread themselves among us. Our man is small and slight, barefoot, and, like everyone here, he is smiling and welcoming.

'My name is Royalty, please follow. I will take you to your beautiful home.' '

Thank you so much. It's nice to meet you. I am Ted, and this is Mary.'

Royalty bows at this news.

'Do you know whether our luggage will be available for collection soon?' Ted asks.

'All luggage is in the room already, sir. If you would like me to unpack it, I can do that immediately and arrange for it to be ironed or cleaned. On this holiday, you will have nothing to worry about. All cares will drift away from you, and you will enjoy the beauty and tranquillity of the island.'

'That's very kind, Thank you. Really - there's no need for you to unpack. I just wanted to check that the luggage had arrived safely.'

'Of course, sir. Of course.'

'I hope you're not going to get too used to being waited on hand and foot,' I tell Ted. He looks terribly pleased with the attention being lavished on him by Royalty.

The walk to the hotel chalets is less than five minutes from the beach. We all walk along - some of us more excited than others: an older couple trundles at a leisurely pace, with the woman holding onto what I assume is her husband's arm; Isabella trots along like a baby giraffe, up on her hooves to avoid her sharp heels from digging into the sand. Her husband looks increasingly annoyed as he carries her bag and her jacket and urges her to speed up.

Ted and I, on the other hand, are fairly skipping along, admiring the view and trying not to squeal with delight. I tell you - everything. I mean, EVERYTHING in this place is as bright and beautiful as the morning sun.

Royalty tells us we have reached our room and points to the French doors, which are wide open and ready for our arrival. He pushes back the voile curtains.

'This is chalet hotel. You can enter by back doors, from the beach, or enter from the main door, which leads into the hotel corridor and down to reception.

'Best of both worlds. Lovely beach at the back and helpful hotel at the front.'

I turn around to admire the view of the sea which stretches out in front of us. Dotted across the ocean are the beautiful white sails of boats and windsurfers - floating like winged creatures atop the waves. To the right are the sumptuous gardens and the swimming pool. Wooden huts are set around the swimming pool. It looks nice there, but not as lovely as the sea view through the French doors.

'This room is called Songbird,' says Royalty, and I swear to God, I've never been happier.

He shows us the gleaming white bathroom with its rainforest shower and spa bath. He shows us the mini bar and explains how the wonderful collection of wooden fans on the ceiling work. He checks whether we want him to unpack for us, then he leaves us in peace, bowing as he exits, closing the door gently behind him.

'Wow,' I say, picking up the brochure lying on the small dressing table. 'Listen to this, Ted: 'There are 30 chalets set in 12 acres of gardens.' No wonder it seems so quiet and relaxed. And the beach we were standing on earlier is a private beach.'

'Amazing,' says Ted. He's lying on the bed, stretching out. I know what he's doing; he does this wherever we go; he's trying to see whether he can lie flat out without his toes going over the edge of the mattress. I ignore him and turn back to the brochure.

'It says we're in the north of the island, near Rodney Bay. There are yoga and Pilates classes and spa treatments using fresh, natural ingredients. I need to get involved in the spa treatments - that sounds lovely.'

'Not the Pilates and yoga classes, though?'

'Na, I'm not so keen on the idea of those. They sound like they might be hard work. I do want to be healthy while we're here, though. It says that all the fruit, vegetables, and spices come from the kitchen garden. Oh, and listen to this - St Lucia is known for its natural beauty and diverse attractions, including the Piton Mountains, a tropical rainforest and one of the world's few drive-in volcanoes. We have to go to that. A drive-through volcano. How cool!'

'OK, enough of that. Come here,' says Ted, dragging me towards him and throwing me onto the bed, which is so soft and bouncy that I rebound into the air before being pinned down by him. 'Are you happy?' he asks.

'No, I'm Mary. Happy is still on the beach,' I say, laughing loudly at my own joke. I have a feeling that jokes about whether I'm feeling happy will punctuate our time away.

Ted sweeps the bags off the bed and eases the straps of my maxi dress down off my shoulders. 'This is coming off now,' he says, in case you were wondering. Then he begins to remove my clothes. '

No, we can't do this. I need a shower,' I say. 'Let me have a shower.'

'I'm helping you. I'm taking off your clothes. And have you noticed how big that shower is? Certainly big enough for two, I'd say.'

'Come on then - let's get dirty then get clean, together.'

Around an hour later (we unpacked as well, Ted's not that good), we are showered, and I'm pondering what to wear for lunch.

'Just wear that blue dress,' says Ted, with all the fashion sense of a rotting banana.

'The midnight blue one? That's not right for lunch,' I say. 'Is there something wrong with you?'

'OK, that black one.' '

Black? For lunch?' I shake my head.

'Well, which one do you want to wear?'

'I want to wear THE DRESS,' I tell him.'

'Oh no - don't start this again,' he says. 'Wear something else. You have 150 dresses in that bag.'

'Yes, but I don't have THE DRESS,' I say mournfully.

Ted slumps onto the bed. 'We're here, in a beautiful hotel, with the sun shining, and you have more clothes in your bag than the entire ladieswear department at Marks and Spencer. For the love of God, put something on and tell me when you're ready, but don't take too long. I'm starving.'

CHAPTER
SIX

OK, I'm sure you're wondering - what is THE DRESS? Let me explain the tragic story. My friend Veronica (you know her - the one I met at Fat Club, and she came on the disastrous trip to Amsterdam with me), well, she was wearing this beautiful orange and pink dress. I know that sounds hideous, but it was gorgeous, and I really wanted it. I assumed it must be expensive, so I reluctantly asked her. She told me that she bought it from Next and it cost £32.

'Bloody hell, I'm going to get one,' I said, pulling out my phone and going onto the Next website. I was delighted to see that one was left in my size, so I dropped it into my basket and bought it immediately. I knew it would be perfect for my trip to St Lucia.

The next day, I received a message from the courier saying it had been delivered. What joy! I swung open the front door to see... no parcel. Nothing at all. What was going on? When I checked the website, it told me the parcel had been delivered, and it even attached a picture of the parcel outside the front door. But when I looked closely, I could see it was someone else's front door. I looked at the neatly pruned trees on either side of the glossy door. It bore no resemblance to my rather scruffy exterior.

I phoned Next and explained my predicament. The man on the phone was incredibly helpful. 'Would you like me to send another one?' he asked. Excellent. Problem solved. But – no - not problem solved at all, because they had run out of the dresses. 'We'll send you a refund,' he said.

'No, I want the dress,' I replied.

'I'm very sorry, but we've run out of them.'

That's when I turned into a raving monster. I put down the receiver and looked back at the picture. Before the phone call, I had been viewing the picture with detached curiosity. Suddenly, I was full-blown Hercule Poirot, determined to find the parcel and wear the dress. Next to the picture of the front door was a map. I clicked on it, and it told me the dress was at April Lodge on Cranmore Street...a mere 10-minute walk. I put Elvis's lead on, and off we went - walking in search of a missing dress. We reached the road, and I pulled out my map, looking carefully to work out where the house was. It was at the far end, so off we trotted, Elvis sniffing and weeing on every doorpost while I looked ahead like I was in the murder squad on the hunt for an armed gangster.

The house was difficult to see, tucked around the corner, right next to the river. I approached the front door and saw the little, heavily groomed trees outside and the glossy door. This was the house. I rang the bell and stood back. What happened next was truly astonishing. A man who looked like he was in his 50s answered the door, and I explained the dilemma...my parcel had been accidentally dropped off at their house.

'Let me check,' he said, calling inside to 'Serena,' who I assumed was his wife.

'Darling, I can't hear you properly. I'm coming now.' I heard the feet padding and saw a lady at the door. She was much younger than the man who had answered, quite heavily pregnant, and...get this...wearing THE DRESS. My dress.

'That's my dress!' I said.

'It's not,' said Serena, backing inside the house. 'It's my dress.'

'It was delivered here by accident.'

'No,' said the woman, hiding out of view.

'That dress is mine. I ordered it, and it was delivered here by mistake.'

'How ridiculous. Shut the door, Simon,' said the woman.

'I'm sorry,' said Simon, turning to me. 'I'm afraid we don't have your dress.'

'Yes, you do...'

But it was no good. The door was firmly shut in my face. What was I to do now? Ring the police? This was theft, plain and simple. The woman should have been jailed.

In the end, I decided the police probably had a lot on their plates, so I decided to ring Ted instead.

'Before I come over there - are you 100% sure,' he said. 'I know what you're like. I'll get there, and we'll discover it's not your dress at all.'

'It's mine,' I said slowly and menacingly. 'You better come now, or things will get ugly.'

'I'm on my way,' he said wearily.

It was as if he didn't quite understand the seriousness of this.

Ted turned up, and we went to knock on the door

together. Simon answered and looked shocked to see me again.

'Stick your foot in the door,' I said to Ted.

'Let me do the talking,' he muttered back.

Then he politely apologised to Simon for disturbing him and said, 'This is very embarrassing, but we know that my wife Mary's dress was left here, and your wife appears to be wearing it. We'd be very grateful if you'd return it. I can leave our address, and you can drop it off at your convenience.'

'No, I want it now,' I said.

'Ssshhhhh...' said Ted.

'I'm afraid there's been some sort of confusion. Serena isn't wearing your wife's dress,' said Simon. 'Perhaps the dresses look alike.'

'Yes, she is, she definitely is,' I said, unable to keep quiet despite Ted's efforts to silence me.

'I assure you I'm not,' said Serena, wafting into view in a different dress entirely.

'Is that the dress?' asked Ted.

'No,' I said. 'She had a different dress on before.'

'What nonsense. Simon, this is the same dress as I was just wearing, isn't it?'

'I, um, yes. I guess,' said Simon, who, in common with most of the men in the world, wouldn't notice if his wife changed dresses every five minutes.

'Look, let me leave you my number, and if you find it, please call us.'

I stood there glowering at them.

'You should have punched him,' I said to Ted.

'I'm not going to punch anyone. Get in the car, and let's go home.'

As we left, Elvis squatted in that dramatic way that dogs do, and pooed all over their driveway.

'Good boy,' I said, climbing into the car. 'You're a good boy.' I have taken him back there for a poo twice since.

So, the upshot of all this is that I have no special orange and pink dress to wear, so I find something in the suitcase; a rather colourful kaftan, and slip it on. Then I brush my hair and shake Ted. 'Come on, let's go and eat,' I say. He jumps up, and we head over to the restaurant for lunch.

Stepping outside is a joy. It's that lovely warmth you only get abroad. The sort of temperature that wraps you up and makes your skin tingle with the deliciousness of it all. The walk to the restaurant takes us through lush gardens full of plants of such variety and colour that I'm forced to stop and admire them all.

'Hey, you like gardens,' says a man in gardening overalls; he has the same wide smile as Happy.

'I'm not much of a gardener, but I work in a gardening centre at home, so I know a little about plants. Ours are nothing like those, though.'

'These are special,' says the gardener. 'The other English girl likes them, too. That girl's gone now, though. I heard people talking.'

'Oh, right,' I say.

The plants are so bright it looks like someone turned the contrast up. One little flower is in the vivid blue you rarely imagine coming from anything but glittery 1980s eyeshadow. It's pure ABBA from the Waterloo days.

We arrive at the restaurant and it turns out that my brightly coloured kaftan is perfect here; everyone is much more dressed up than at home. No one is wearing black, so I'm glad I paid no heed to the terrible fashion advice from Stylist Ted. They all favour pinks, sky blues and an alarmingly bright neon green colour. I feel right among them as I float around the room in my dress made from a material as fine as butterflies' wings, in the colours of a peacock's feather.

'Can I introduce myself?' says a tall, blonde woman.

I guess she's around my age, but unlike me, she has a cut-glass English accent. She looks like she might be related to Isabella; with the same ethereal glow.

'My name's Amelia, and I am the manager here.'

'Oh, how nice to meet you,' I say. I notice Ted looking at her, mesmerised. She's arrestingly beautiful, with golden tresses cascading past her shoulders in waves, framing a face of porcelain perfection. With a delicate motion, she raises her slender hand to tuck an errant strand behind her ear.

'What a beautiful hotel you have here,' I say, feeling dumpy and unattractive in her presence.

'Thank you. If you want anyone to show you around or help - just let us know, won't you? Ah - here's Happy. I'm sure you've met him.'

'Hello, hello, my friends. You look so good, my lady. Look at you all dressed up like a hummingbird.'

'Thank you, Happy, that's just the look I was going for.'

He kisses me on the cheek and tells Ted how lucky he is.

'I am,' Ted says, with a nod. 'I'm the luckiest man in the world.'

Happy cheers at that remark - a loud, barrelling cheer that develops into a laugh that causes everyone in the restaurant to look around, but once they see it's just Happy being Happy, they turn back to their food.

'Why don't you join us for lunch,' says Ted. 'We're just

going to sit over there in the sunshine. Amelia, we'd love you to join us, too.'

'I wish I could, but I have some issues here to sort out. I'm sure Happy will entertain you.'

'Of course, I would love to join you. I'll just make sure everyone is seated, and I'll come and tell you about this place.'

Ted and I head for the sunniest table with a view of the sea. We can see the watersports hut on the beach and loads of lovely boats dotted across the waves.

We scan the menu before us. There's a wide range of dishes, including every sea creature you can imagine, and more conventional burgers, steaks, and fish' n' chips.

'Or there's a crazy-nice food bar,' says Happy, joining us. 'It has everything on it.'

'It has everything? That's the sort of food I like.'

I jump up and head for the main counter. Happy isn't wrong. There's a delicious mix of healthy exotic fruit, salads and vegetables, stews, pies, meats and a wide variety of potatoes - from chips to dauphinoise and everything in between.

I put some chips and dauphinoise on my plate, then cover them with a fresh green salad. No one needs to know what lurks beneath the lettuce. There are some lovely pieces of barbecue chicken which I reach to pick up, but then I think of all the chickens at the airport and swiftly put them down. I opt for lobster and saltfish instead and head back to the table.

As I sit down, Ted stands up to get his food.

'Have you ever been to England?' I ask Happy.

He moves his head slowly from side to side. 'Never been, but I know exactly what it's like there.'

'What do you think it's like there?' I ask.

Happy sips his drink and smiles as he speaks. 'It's like Downton Abbey. People walking about in bowler hats and drinking tea.'

'Yeah, that's pretty much it,' I say. 'It's quite nice not to have to wear the bowler hat today, to be honest.'

'You've got small cars too, haven't you?' he says. 'Much smaller cars than the Americans have.'

'Yes,' I agree. 'But the Americans drive cars that are bigger than my house. We just drive cars that people fit into.'

'And the food in England is terrible, isn't it? You guys like eating terrible food.'

'Actually, you can get some really lovely food in England now,' says Ted, taking his seat. 'There are Caribbean restaurants, Italian restaurants, French restaurants...every type of restaurant you like. English food is good now.'

I stop myself from pointing out that he's just listed a load of non-English restaurants, which doesn't exactly prove his point.

'You know the thing I really like about England, though,' says Happy, nodding his head and smiling to himself, his eyes closed against the glare of the sun. 'You play cricket. There's a lot to like about a country that plays cricket. Do you play?'

Ted explains that he used to play a lot when he was younger, and that he also played rugby. The respect with which Happy looks at him is out of this world.

'Did you play for England?'

'No, I played for a rugby club called Harlequins.'

'No, not the rugby. I don't care about rugby; I only care about cricket. Did you play cricket for England? Have you ever met Darren Sammy?'

'No, just a social player; I've never met Darren Sammy.'

'He's my hero. I'd love to meet Mr Sammy. The greatest human being ever. I have a sticker on my pick truck which says 'I love Darren Sammy.'

' I smile at Happy as his grin becomes wider and his face dreamier as he thinks of his hero.

'It must be lovely living here,' I say to Happy.

'Best place on earth.'

'Were you born here?'

'Yes. I'm St Lucian through and through. My parents and grandparents are all from the island. They worked hard to look after us all. I was a raggedy child – always playing – I spent every spare moment on the beach or in the water.'

'Was your dad in the hotel business?'

'No, no. He was a fisherman. He died when I was very young. It was difficult, but we are OK now.'

'I'm sorry to hear that. Does your mum live near here?'

'In Castries, just across the island. I haven't moved far, have I?'

'I wouldn't if I lived here,' I say. 'It seems so perfect'

'I guess nowhere's perfect, but it's pretty good.'

While we're talking, I surreptitiously eat the chips from underneath the lettuce. I'm hoping that Happy thinks I'm eating lettuce. I don't know why. Why am I doing this? Why don't I just eat them normally?

Ted returns after a second trip to the food bar, and sits down with a huge plate of stew, rice and chips.

'Any advice for us, then?' Ted asks. 'Things we should and shouldn't do while we're here?'

'I'll let you have some information about all the trips you can take and all the places you can visit. There's a lot to do here.

'Main advice about what you shouldn't do? Don't get in

trouble with the police. They are not like the police you have at home. They are corrupt, they take money, and they are lazy.'

'Oh right, we'll try not to break any laws then,' I say.

But Happy's not up for joking about it.

'Yes. Be careful. We've all fallen on the wrong side of their violence before. But – hey – don't worry – they won't bother you. Tell me what sort of holiday you want, and I will let you have all the information you need.'

'I want to laze around, see some beautiful sights and I fancy having a go at windsurfing. I'll probably be rubbish, but I wouldn't mind trying.'

'You won't be rubbish - you'll be great. I run the water-sports hut and all the trainers there, so I'll find someone great to look after you. Tom's good. I can fix up a lesson with Tom if you would like?'

'That would be amazing. Thank you, Happy,' I say.

Ted is looking off into the distance while we talk. I instinctively follow his gaze.

'Look, there are police everywhere down there.' Ted points down to the seafront, where police have gathered near the watersports hut.

'Blimey, there are loads of them.'

'See you later,' says Happy, leaping over the side of the balustrade and belting off through the gardens in the opposite direction from the seafront.

'Blimey - he doesn't like the police, does he?' I say as our new friend disappears.

He's out of sight in no time; the happy smile and billowing pink shorts are gone for now.

CHAPTER SEVEN

As darkness descends in St Lucia, it does so suddenly. One minute, it's light and sunny; the next, it's pitch black. It's not like at home where the sunlight ebbs away slowly like a balloon deflating. Here, someone sticks a pin in the balloon, and it's gone instantly as if there's been a sudden raid on the light.

It's a bit of a shame because Ted and I plan to picnic on the beach tonight instead of the more formal dining experience in the restaurant. We've decided upon some 'we' time, away from the other couples. They all seem nice, but this holiday is about spending time together, and I don't want to listen to all the trials and tribulations of Isabella's 100-metre loft conversion and how she keeps her weight below three stone. Not tonight.

So, here we are then, in the darkness, walking hand-in-hand along the beach. It's dark but pleasant after the balmy weather in the afternoon, and I love the feeling of warm sand between my toes as Ted and I amble towards the rocks. The ocean laps gently beside us. I feel like I'm starring in a travel brochure.

Ted has a basket containing our food for the evening that the guys in the restaurant have prepared. They've also given him a large blanket and a lovely bottle of champagne.

'Why don't we sit over there?' Ted points out the area on the far side of the beach, where the water sports are based during the day but which lies empty in the evenings. The area benefits from a glow from the lamp on the top of the water sports hut next to the craggy rocks. The illumination from the hut creates a pool of light on the sand.

Once we get to the bright spot, Ted busies himself with laying out the blanket and placing the food and drink on it. I stand there, almost mesmerised by the lovely feeling underfoot; the exfoliating grains of sand push up between my toes as I wriggle them around.

When I work in the garden centre, I wear big boots to keep my feet warm. They are good boots, to be fair: sturdy enough so that if plant pots or ladders fall on them, you won't break your toes, but it means the feeling of having my feet free, walking barefoot and feeling grains of sand between my toes is all the more lovely on holiday. It's like a mini pedicure.

'What on earth are you doing?' asks Ted, unloading a large salad, a giant slab of focaccia bread and a glorious bowl of prawns. 'You have a very strange look on your face.'

'The sand is massaging my feet. It feels lovely.'

'Well, I'll be in charge of the food, then, and you carry on wriggling your toes in that odd manner. Do you want this blanket over your shoulders?'

'I'm OK,' I say. 'Still nice and warm, isn't it?'

'Yeah, I think it will turn quite cold soon though, now that the sun's gone in.'

Ted continues to rummage through the bag. 'Oh look, there's a desert here as well, and a canister of coffee and some warm milk to go with it, along with a selection of gorgeous chocolate biscuits and cheesecake. Look at this cheesecake...'

'Yum,' I reply. The food all looks great, but I'm enjoying my foot exfoliation too much to go over there. I push my foot deep into the sand...then I feel something against my foot.

'Something's in here,' I say. 'I can't work out what it is.'

I pull my foot out and peer into the hole in the sand. I can't see anything, so I push my foot back into it.

I can feel it again.

'What if it's a crab? Can you help me, Ted? Oh God, what is it? Perhaps it's a lobster. This place is called Lobster Bay. I bet it's a lobster.'

Ted walks over to me and looks down at the sand. 'I can't see anything,' he says. 'Does it hurt?'

'No, it doesn't hurt... I can just feel it. I'm scared to pull my foot out in case it's got me clamped.'

'Well, I'll pull it out for you,' says Ted, reaching down, grabbing my ankle, and yanking it out of the sand. I go tumbling backwards and land in a heap, my toe in the air, completely unscathed.

'Are you okay?' Ted leans over and gives me his hand. I take it and pull myself upright, almost pulling him down next to me, comedy-style, in the process.

'I'm fine. What's there?' I ask.

'I'm not sure I want to look,' says Ted, kicking aggressively at the point where my toe had been in the sand. 'There is something in there. Perhaps it's a rock.'

'No, it was sharp. It has teeth,' I say.

He leans over and peers at the sand, his face screwed up in concentration. 'Oh yes, I can see it. It's black with gold teeth at the front. It looks like some sort of rat.'

'What the hell, Ted? How can you say that so calmly? What do you mean - some sort of rat? Do you think it's dangerous? I don't think it bit me or anything.'

'Maybe not a rat, but it's like some sort of woodland creature. Do they have water moles or otters here?'

'What? In the sand?'

We move cautiously towards it, both of us peering over, trying to get the best view possible without disturbing the creature buried in the sand.

'I think it's dead,' I say. 'It is difficult to see anything in this darkness, but I can make out something, and it isn't moving.'

'I know what we need,' says Ted, retrieving his mobile phone from the depths of his pockets and turning on the light. He shines it down onto the beach.

'You idiot,' he says. 'It's just a purse; it was the clasp sticking into you.'

'Don't call me an idiot... You were ranting on about otters.'

'OK, fair enough. I was a bit of a wimp. But you did say there was a creature there.'

'I wonder who it belongs to.'

Ted picks it up and dusts the sand off it as we walk over and sit on the blanket, the magnificent spread of food momentarily and unusually pushed to the backs of our minds.

'It's a very large purse,' I say.

It's leather with a gold ornamental clasp on the front, and it is stuffed so full that the zip across the top is stretched so the teeth look as if they are going to break apart.

'I wonder why it was buried so deeply?'

'Do you think it's been there for years and years?

Perhaps it washed in from a shipwrecked boat in the 16th century?' I venture.

'It seems unlikely,' says Ted. 'It looks quite modern. It says 'Zara' on it. Did they have Zara in the 16th century?'

'No. It was just Topshop back then.'

'Maybe we should check with Happy when we get back to the hotel. One of the guests might have lost it.'

'Yes,' I say, leaning over to cut off a piece of cheesecake. I can't leave this food in front of me, uneaten, however fascinating our discovery.

'Is there a name inside it? Perhaps a business card or something,' asks Ted. 'You better look. I was told that a gentleman should never look in a lady's purse.'

'Yes, good idea. This cheesecake is delicious, by the way, really lovely. Make sure you have some.'

The cake has a tangy lime coating on the creamy middle and a thick biscuit base that looks solid and gives a good crunch. I lean over to have another piece. I can see Ted watching me.

'What's the matter?'

'The purse - open the purse. Oh, sod it, I'm going in. Don't tell my dad I looked into a ladies' purse.'

And he opens it.

'Shit. Fuck. My God, Mary - look.'

The purse is full of money - a huge wad of notes fills the bag. Modern money. Today's money. All in US dollars.'

'Oh My God. Ted, what do you think it's for?'

'I've no idea.'

'I've never seen so much money,' I say, stopping mid-bite and looking at Ted.

'Why would anyone leave all this money on the beach?'

As Ted speaks, I instinctively look around, eagerly scanning the horizon lest someone is watching us. I see a brief movement on the rocks, but it's nothing more than birds swooping into the light next to us.

'There are thousands and thousands of dollars in there,' I say, needlessly. 'What are we going to do with it? Is there anything to indicate whose it is?'

'There doesn't seem to be anything in there other than cash. No credit cards, no driving license, none of the usual paraphernalia. Let's check properly when we get back to the room. I don't want to pull all that money out here.'

'There must be about $5,000 in there?' I say to Ted.

'And the rest. I honestly think there could be $7000. This is weird.'

'I know. Shall we head back? I don't feel comfortable with it here. Let's just tell reception and get them to call the police.'

'Oh, hang on... There's something in here.'

Ted pulls out a piece of paper and unfolds it.

'It's got the name Cara Jeffries written on the top, and It's an invitation to a party aboard one of the boats in the harbour...

'*You are invited to join us aboard Omeros for champagne, canapes and dancing.*'

'Wow. That sounds nice. When's the party?'

'Tomorrow night.'

'Tomorrow?'

'Yes - that's what it says.'

'So, it must have been left here fairly recently?' I suggest.

'Yeah, I suppose. Come on, let's head back.'

'We could always turn up at the boat tomorrow night. She might invite us to stay for the party.'

'No, we're not doing anything like that. We're taking it

to the police, not going to some strange party with thousands of pounds in my back pocket.'

'We can't do that; you heard what Happy said. The police are all completely corrupt here.'

'No, that's not what he said; he said that some of the police are corrupt; I'm sure some are very upstanding and sensible.'

'I think he said all of them. But, in any case, we need to give that wallet back to the person who owns it without involving dodgy policemen, and we know that the person who owns it will be on the boat tomorrow night.'

'Yeah, maybe,' said Ted. 'Hopefully, it belongs to someone at the hotel; then, we won't have to go traipsing off to find them.'

I know this might sound weird, but I hoped that no one at the hotel would know who the wallet's owner was because I fancied going to a boat party and playing detective. I was intrigued about why there was so much money in it. Perhaps it was something boring like a down payment for a mortgage or a car or something? Or perhaps it was something altogether more intriguing, criminal perhaps.

'Are you not going to eat any of this food?' I say to Ted. I've made quite a dent in the collection of desserts, but he's had nothing.

'I can't eat. I just want to get back to the hotel,' he says. This is most unlike him. The two of us are usually absolute gannets, eating everything within a few feet of us.

'OK, let's just finish our wine and go.'

The purse lies on the blanket between us as we drink. I occasionally glance at it, burdened by its sudden presence in our lives.

'Come on, let's go,' says Ted, and I jump up and follow him across the sand to the hotel.

By the time we arrive back at reception, it's late. A night receptionist is working, someone we've never met before. The idea of handing thousands of pounds over feels wrong.

'Is Happy around?' I ask.

'He's not here now. He'll be back at the water sports hut tomorrow morning. Can I help with anything? Or can I get Royalty to attend to you?' the man asks.

'It's OK,' I say, looking at Ted. 'Shall we catch up with him tomorrow?'

Ted nods, and we walk back to the room, neither of us speaking. Ted keeps his hand on his shorts pocket, protecting its contents with all his might.

As soon as we are alone in the chalet, I realise how worried Ted is. He goes through a huge performance of locking the door and pushing an armchair against it.

'Honest to God, Ted. What are you doing?'

'I've got thousands of dollars in my pocket,' he said. 'I can't just leave it lying around on the sideboard. It doesn't hurt to be cautious.'

I shake my head as Ted continues to move furniture around, heaving heavy chests of drawers so they stand in front of the door while I shut the blinds and pull the feathery light curtains across.

'It's a lot of money,' he says, seeing the confusion on my face as he rushes around like a lunatic.

'I know it's a lot of money. And if people knew we had lots of money in here, I'd understand your fears. But no one knows we've got the purse; no one knows that we've got thousands of dollars sitting here. No one is going to break in looking for it because I don't know we have it.'

'It's better to be safe than sorry,' says Ted, sounding exactly like my mum.

Cautiously, he lifts the purse out of his pocket and

places it on the bed as if it were an unexploded bomb. We both look at it.

'Shall we count how much money is in there?' I say.

Ted looks doubtful.

'I think we should check it.'

Ted continues to look doubtful.

How come I am so much nosier than him?

'It was dark on the beach, Ted. We could easily have missed something.'

'OK. Yes, you're right; we should look inside. I'm just trying to be sensible. It's not our property; it's a lot of money, and we're staying in a strange place. Oh - and the police are violent lunatics. I'd rather we were cautious with it. But you're right; we should check it properly.'

I need no more encouragement than that. Before he finishes his sentence, I have tipped the purse's contents onto the bed. Money cascades out; the invitation to the boat party is among the notes. It looks like a glitzy and gorgeous party and part of me longs to go there to find the owner.

While I'm picturing myself aboard a magnificent yacht, Ted takes the notes and counts them, flowing through the notes with his fat fingers before declaring:

'There is $11,000 in the wallet. Who on earth has $11,000 in their purse? I mean – who? Not even the richest man in the world needs to carry that sort of cash around. What do you need cash for? Everywhere I go, I just tap my credit card. Why would anyone have this amount of cash in a purse? Normal people don't.'

'Let me look if there's anything else in the pockets,' I say, taking the purse and going through every slit in the leather until I come across a tiny pocket on the inside. I push my finger into it and pull out a key. It is tiny. So small that I can't imagine what on earth it fits. Perhaps a jewellery box?

We both look at the key for minutes, neither of us speaking. Then I feel around a bit more in the small pockets and pull out a tiny note with the smallest map on it. I pull out my phone and take a picture, enlarging it to see what it says.

It's a map of the main St Lucia Central railway station with a tiny '7' marked on the side, right by the ladies' toilets, in the departures terminal.

'What does all this mean?' asks Ted.

'I don't know. But tomorrow, we are going on that boat to find out.'

CHAPTER

EIGHT

When I wake the next morning, it isn't to the gentle sounds of exotic birds singing prettily overhead, but to the roar of Ted, fast asleep next to me, snoring like a giant pig. I look over at him sprawled across the sheets, his face all contorted into a strange shape as he copes with the events of his dream, occasionally murmuring and screwing up his nose still further, but all the while keeping up the extraordinary noise levels.

Then I remember.

The purse.

The huge amount of money.

The boat party.

Feelings of excitement rise inside me. We're going to the boat party tonight to find Cara, to reunite her with her purse.

I wonder where the boat is? I reach over to my phone and turn the screen on, hoping the bright light won't wake Ted. I call up a map of St Lucia; it's such a small island that most of it is on the coast. I glance down the island's west side but can't remember where the boat is moored.

I creep out of bed and over towards the safe, stumbling over the furniture that Ted had moved around for our 'safety' the night before. Ted makes a strange throaty sigh, so I stop in my tracks and stand very still. Then the snoring starts again, so I creep like a cat burglar over to the safe. I put in the code and peer inside. I am half expecting there to be no purse there and to discover that I dreamed the whole thing.

But there it is.

Black purse; gold clasp.

Stuffed full of money.

I pull it gently from the safe and start to undo it.

'What are you doing?' says Ted, sitting up in bed.

Bugger. Bugger, bugger.

'Nothing. I just want to look at the name of the boat where the party is tonight and see whether I can work out where it is on the map.'

'I think it's at a place called Marigold,' says Ted. 'Do you need to know now? At this time in the morning?'

'I couldn't sleep. And - yes, Marigold rings a bell,' I say as I unzip the purse and take out the invitation.

'Here it is - Marigot Bay Marina. I wonder where on earth that is.'

I get back into bed and pick up my phone. 'Right, so we are here, near Rodney Bay. That's Pigeon Island there. Do you remember the coach driver was talking about it when he drove us here, it's just north of us. Marigot Bay is further south. Oh, listen to what they say about it on the internet:

Marigot Bay is the most beautiful bay in the Caribbean Sea.'

'Wow. Sounds good. Nice place to moor your boat for a party. Perhaps we should go to the boat, return the purse, and then go to dinner there. There must be lots of waterside restaurants,' says Ted.

'We could do that or see whether we can stay on the boat and go to the party. I'm dying to find out more about Cara.'

'Christ, you're loving this, aren't you?'

'Kind of. I think it's intriguing. I want to know what it's all about. Aren't you intrigued?'

'I'm just desperate to return it, love. I don't like the idea of wandering around the place with all that money on me.'

'But you must be a bit intrigued,' I say, jumping on top of him and straddling him. 'I mean - who has that sort of money? And - more importantly - who has that sort of money and leaves it lying on the beach? She must be panicking like mad that she's lost it.'

Ted turns me on my back so it's him on top. 'You should have been a detective,' he says, kissing my neck. 'Detective Inspector Mary Brown reporting for duty.'

Then he kisses me again, down my neck, twisting his tongue under the thin straps of my nightdress, pulling them down over my shoulder, over my elbows and down to my waist.

'You are beautiful,' he says, as he begins kissing me in all sorts of places that I shall not mention for fear of making you blush. The kissing continues, then it develops, and it's just Ted and me in the Caribbean, making love on a bed as soft as clouds while the sun peeks through the blinds opposite us and warms our naked bodies. I feel like I'm on the set of some wonderful romance film.

We lie there after our exertions, happy and exhausted, until Ted says the three magic words.

'Fancy some breakfast?'

. . .

We take our 'usual' table on the veranda before heading up to see what's available for breakfast. It's a real feast for the senses...a colourful array of fruits on one side of a giant trestle table and the glorious, unbeatable smell of cooked English breakfast on the other, between the two sit cheeses, meats, granola pots, yoghurt and delicious breads and cakes. I look over at Ted, and he's got so much on his plate I think it's all going to go toppling off; it's as if a toddler has been let loose.

'I think I'm going to need a considerably bigger plate,' he says as he passes me, taking banana bread and a brioche bun in his left hand because there is no room on the plate he's carrying in his right.

My plate which is, itself, brimming with food, makes me look positively abstemious in comparison.

We sit down, and I lift my face to the sky. The sun is already warm; I should have put on sunscreen. I'll have to remember to put it on every time I come out. I'm not the sort of person who tans well. When I went on holiday a few years ago, I practically glowed crimson, bordering on radioactive. To the friends who were with me, I have become a cautionary tale about the importance of frequent sunscreen application.

'Excuse me, I'm so sorry to bother you.' I look up to see Amelia standing there. She is dressed in a beautiful green dress which hugs her figure, making her look slimmer than ever.

'Hi Amelia, how nice to see you.'
'Are you enjoying yourselves?'
'Oh, very much - it's like paradise.'
'I'm so glad. If you need anything at all, just ask. We

want you to have the best time imaginable.'

'Thank you, and thank you for the picnic last night; it was perfect.'

'Oh, I'm so glad. Look, I have a bit of a favour to ask you...when you've finished breakfast, and there's no rush at all, would you mind having a quick chat with these gentlemen here?'

She indicates three men sitting at a table in the far corner.

'I've asked them to wait until you've finished eating. They're police officers. Nothing to worry about, but there was a bit of an incident on the beach last night, and they wondered whether you saw anything when you were having your picnic.'

'Of course, that's no problem,' says Ted, as I look down at my food, trying not to give away the fact that we did indeed see something last night: a purse containing over ten grand.

Amelia thanks us profusely and walks back over to where the policemen are based.

I look at Ted.

'Fuck,' I say. 'What the hell shall we do?'

'We'll tell them what we found and explain that we plan to take it to Cara tonight on the boat. If they want to take it off us, that's up to them.'

'But what about everything that Happy said - that the police can't be trusted?'

'I don't know, Mary. But I know we need to extricate ourselves from this complicated situation as quickly as possible.'

'But we've done nothing wrong.'

'Exactly, we haven't done anything wrong, but if we start lying to the police, we will have done something wrong.'

'But what if the policeman who speaks to us looks dodgy?'

'Then I guess we won't mention the money. We'll tell Happy what happened and see what he suggests.'

'But then we'll have lied to the police,' I say.

This has all become terribly confusing.

'Let's just take it one step at a time. We'll eat our breakfast, then go over there.'

We finish our breakfasts quietly until I remember something.

'You know what I've just thought of...there were police here yesterday. Do you remember? They were over by the water sports hut, and Happy ran off when he saw them.'

'Yes, of course I remember.'

'Well - maybe there's something else going on. The police yesterday had nothing to do with the purse because we hadn't even found it then.'

'Oh, it could be. Perhaps they are just talking to everyone. Let's relax for now. This is our honeymoon. I want you to enjoy it.'

I'll be honest: I eat extra slowly because I can't bear the idea of talking to police officers. Not because they scare me but because I am worried that Ted will hand over the purse and deny me the chance to meet Cara and learn about her, the missing money, and the exciting key.

Eventually, I can't put it off any longer. I've eaten my body weight in mango. It's time to talk to the police. Ted stands up and heads for the table at the back of the room, and I follow him.

We are introduced to three uniformed officers. The main guy looks like a gangster from a Guy Ritchie movie. His name is Victor Emanuel, and he tells us with great pride that he is the Assistant Superintendent of Police. He looks like a man who has never suffered from a lack of confidence. 'This is Augustin, Henry and William.' All three nod.

'We just want to check something with you. We're asking all the guests. Did you, by any chance, go to the beach last night or see anything strange? Amelia thought you might have walked along the beach before your picnic?'

While one guy talks, the other two stare aggressively.

'We went for a picnic on the beach last night. It was dark, so we didn't see anything, and it was quite cold, so we came back. We were only there for half an hour at the most,' I say.

'Where did you have the picnic?' asks the angry guy.

'Sort of near the rocks,' says Ted.

'Sort of? What does sort of mean?'

Ted looks up abruptly. 'Well, I can't give you ordnance survey coordinates, but we were quite near the rocks.'

'Why go to the beach at all?' the angry officer asks me.

'We thought it would be romantic.' I say.

'Did you see anything unusual?' asked Augustin. None of them except Victor had spoken until this point.

'No. We just had a picnic on the beach. After the picnic, we came back. What's the problem?'

'Were you anywhere near the water sports hut?'

'Yes, we were quite near there. We thought it was a good spot because there was light from the hut.'

'Light? What, the lights were on?'

'No. Well, I don't know whether the lights were on inside, but the light on the outside was on. It didn't give much light, but it gave some.'

'The light outside the hut is only on when the lights inside are on.'

'Right. Well, I guess the lights were on inside then.'

The officer glared at me like he didn't believe a word I was saying. Ted hadn't mentioned the purse, so neither would I. These guys were so aggressive.

'Why are you asking all these questions?'

'When the manager went down there to open up the water sports hut this morning, the entire beach had been dug up; the beach is a mess. This is the latest development in a case we're working on, so we need all the help we can get.'

'Blimey. There was no sign of that when we were there,' I say, but I'm feeling nervous now... should I mention the purse? This could be connected. Then I look at their angry faces and decide that I want to talk to Happy first, then I'll know which are the good guys and which aren't.'

'Thank you for your time. Where are you going now?'

'Back to the room.'

'Can we accompany you?'

'You can, but if you want to come into our chalet, tell me what you want. We have told you everything we know.'

'I just want to see where your chalet is and where you walked last night.'

'Sure,' says Ted.

We walk along the beach route to the room, all in silence. Two police officers stand behind Ted and me as we open the door while Victor stands on the sand next to us. Ted pushes, and furniture scrapes across the floor. He pushes again, but the door hardly opens.

'Is there a problem?' asks Victor.

'No,' says Ted. 'Everything's fine here. Just a bit of trouble getting in. Is there anything else you'd like us to help with?'

'We need to know where you walked last night as part of our efforts to determine when the trouble occurred and where the assailants came from. But what's preventing you from going into the room?'

'We moved some furniture around,' says Ted. 'Nothing to worry about.'

'Moved it around? Against the door?'

Victor glances at one of the other officers. I suddenly feel wildly guilty about not being honest but frozen into continuing with the deception because I don't trust them an inch. I feel like we are too far into the whole thing to say, 'Oh, also, we found over ten grand in the sand.'

'I'll show you where we walked,' says Ted, leading the motley crew towards the water sport hut.

While they hunt for footprints in the sand or whatever else they are doing, an officer stands on the sand outside my back door as if on guard.

'Everything OK?' comes a voice from the next chalet.

Oh God. Not him. It's Barney, the guy we met at the airport, coming out of his chalet with Isabella hot on his heels, dressed for a business meeting in Manhattan. What is it with the pencil skirts and jackets in this weather?

'Everything's fine, thanks. I didn't realise you two were next door.'

'Yes, right here. If these chaps are bothering you, let me know. I used to be in the police, you know. I was very senior. They shouldn't be hassling you about this nonsense on the beach last night. The police here can be very amateurish.'

'Oh, you know about that?'

'Yes - Amelia mentioned it at breakfast. She said you were the only ones on the beach last night.'

'We were, but I think the trouble was much later.'

'Indeed. Well, as I say - be careful about this lot; they

don't have the best of reputations - and let me know if I can help.'

'Thank you. I will.'

I am about to let myself into the room when Ted comes striding over. 'Come on, let's go inside,' he says.

We close and lock the door and sit down on the bed.

'Christ.' I drop my head into my hands.

'We should have told them about the purse,' Ted says.

'I thought you would.'

'I should have. We should go to the police station and tell them.'

'I don't know. Barney came out while you were walking down the beach with PC Plod. He said the police here have a bad reputation.'

'Are you suggesting that we talk to Barney about the money?'

'No, God no. We take the money to the boat tonight and if there are any further problems, we go straight to the police.'

'This is insane,' says Ted. 'Why would someone dig up the whole beach?'

'Because they are looking for the purse?'

'Oh God, no. Don't say that.'

THAT AFTERNOON, the rain came - fast torrents pouring down on the beautiful sun-soaked island. Then the sun reappeared - smiling down on us as if it had never been gone.

The weather was remarkable. One minute, the sun blazed in a cloudless sky, turning the pavement into a sizzling griddle. The next minute, dark storm clouds swept in like a gang of bullies, ready to unleash their fury.

'Come on then,' said Ted. 'Let's go to the boat to find Cara.'

CHAPTER NINE

Cara's story: 14th June
THREE WEEKS EARLIER

CARA STOOD ON THE SAND, watching the sun sparkling on the sea, while a group of children screamed excitedly behind her. They were being fitted with lifejackets so that Cara could take them out for a sailing class. Tom ensured the children were safely strapped in before joining her to drag the small boats towards the water's edge.

'Look, I wanted to apologise for the whole thing with the guys the other day. You know – at lunch – when we were talking about them taking photos of you when you were out on the water. They didn't mean any harm at all. They're rough around the edges, but they're good guys. They aren't used to working with a woman.'

Cara smiled. 'I don't mind, really, as long as they realise I know what I'm doing. You can be female and very competent.'

'Yes. They know that. They were only joking around. They were like that when I started as well. They're a lovely bunch of guys though.'

'Yes, I get that impression. Now, come on then, let's teach this rabble how to sail,' said Cara.

Tom smiled warmly at her as they gathered the excited children around the boats and told them the basics of sailing. Cara showed them how to rig the sails, pointing out the different parts and their functions. The children listened intently, their eyes wide with curiosity.

As they set out onto the water, Cara and Tom worked together, each taking a small group of children under their wing. Cara patiently guided her young sailors, teaching them how to read the wind and adjust the sails accordingly. She demonstrated the proper techniques for steering the boat, her hands gently guiding theirs as they took turns at the helm.

After the session, they wiped down the boats and tied them up so they were ready for the afternoon sessions, then returned to the hut.

The hut was packed with water sports equipment; sleek, modern windsurfing boards lined one wall, their sails rolled up and secured, waiting to catch the perfect gust of wind. A collection of well-maintained sailing dinghies and catamarans stood beside the opposite wall. In the hut's centre, shelves were stocked with an array of water sports accessories. Brightly coloured life jackets in various sizes hung from hooks. Wetsuits were neatly folded and stacked, while a huge basket housed snorkels, masks, and fins.

Cara eased her way around the storage area where kayaks and stand-up paddleboards were stored. She collected her rucksack.

'Do you fancy lunch? My treat?' said Tom.

Cara would have loved to have had a leisurely lunch with him, but Tajo was on his way, and she needed to get back to make herself look as glamorous as possible before his arrival.

'Another time?' she suggested.

∽

'More suncream?'

'Oh yes, please. The sun is very hot,' said Cara.

Tajo laughed as he rubbed suncream into her back.

'Why are you laughing?'

'Well, you English saying 'the sun is very hot' It's the funniest thing ever. Of course, the sun is hot. The sun is about ten thousand degrees.'

'But you know what I mean...in England, it can be sunny, and you can only just about take your coat off, but over here, when it's sunny, it burns through to the centre of your soul.'

'The sun is beautiful,' he said. 'But not as beautiful as you.'

Cara felt swaddled in love and kindness.

'No one has ever been as sweet to me as you are.'

'Then you have not met the right person before. You and I are meant to be together. I want to come to England when you leave. I never want us to be apart. I want to be with you forever.'

Cara felt herself glow with delight. This man was such a joy to be around. He'd done so much for her since she arrived.

When she'd told him she wanted to decorate her hut, he'd been there in a flash, eager to take her to the shops to buy what she needed. He even offered decorating tips.

'Mum was an interior designer. I know a thing or two about this,' he had joked.

Then, while she was on the ocean, teaching water sports to crowds of visitors, he had busied himself painting, varnishing and cleaning until the place looked amazing. She'd only just met him, but she'd never felt like this before. She'd grown so close to him that he had sent all thoughts of Dean spinning out of her mind...something she never imagined happening.

Cara touched his hand affectionately. She was enjoying their wonderful, all-in relationship. He was tender, kind, and warm. Sometimes, they'd go on dates to parts of the island she was unfamiliar with, and other times they'd stay in her hut. Late at night, they would go for walks when the beach was empty and sneak behind the windsurfing hut to kiss like teenagers.

'Come on,' he said. 'I want to take you somewhere wonderful. Fancy lunch?'

'Yum, yes, please.'

They headed off in Tajo's car to a beautiful little restaurant near a beach just south of Lobster Bay. He took Cara's hand and led her up the rickety stone steps carved into the side of the rocks. Turquoise waters splashed beneath them as they giggled like schoolchildren.

'Hello,' said Tajo, high-fiving one of the waiters. 'This is my beautiful girlfriend, Cara.'. The waiter bowed and kissed her hand.

Girlfriend? It felt wonderful when he said that.

They were led to a table on the far side of the bistro, with the best views over the cliff top and out to sea. The sun beamed down, the sea radiated its brilliance, and a handsome man in a white shirt was pouring the wine.

As the wine waiter withdrew, Tajo turned to Cara. 'I'm

so pleased you came into my life. I don't remember the last time I was this happy.'

'Me neither.'

'Good. I'm glad. You are a very special lady. If there is ever anything you need, you only have to ask.'

'There is something I need...I need to know everything about you. I want you to tell me something about yourself that I don't already know,' said Cara.

'Well, my favourite colour is yellow.'

'OK. Anything else? Perhaps something with a bit more depth? I want you to tell me all about yourself from childhood to the present day...'

'Wow, that's a big ask. OK, well - I didn't have the best of childhoods, I guess. Dad wasn't very fatherly. And that's a pretty big understatement. Dad was a troublemaker. He was never there. I had to fend for myself a lot.

'I did OK at school, though. Not as well as you did, but I didn't do bad. I just got in with the wrong people. Not people like you. People who are on the wrong side of the law.

'Oh no. That sounds tough.'

'I managed to escape that life. Through all the clever investments, I made enough money to move out of the area and start up again somewhere else.'

His gaze was intense, and as he leaned in to kiss her, it was more forceful than his kisses had been before.

'My place?' he said.

'Your place.'

Tajo lived near the restaurant, just a short walk through the vibrant hibiscus bushes. Their flowers yielded a wonderful scent that would always remind Cara of this moment.

'Here we are,' he said, pointing out a beautiful white house in the hills. The place was spectacular - a giant detached mansion surrounded by lush gardens with stunning views of the beach below. She could see the swimming pool glistening at the front of the house.

'How long have you lived here?'

'For the last five years. Since the business started taking off.'

'You're very clever to understand investments and financial stuff. I'm hopeless.'

'There's not much to understand.'

'I'm terrible. I was never great at maths at school. Numbers baffle me.'

'I'm not great either, but with this Lajan scheme, I have managed to quadruple my money and life's never been the same. I just keep reinvesting, and my money grows. I have a few homes now, but this is my favourite. It's not the most expensive, but the views are astonishing.'

'It looks beautiful,' she said, walking towards it. If this wasn't the most expensive, some of the houses he owned must be incredible. He took her hand, and they walked to the gate at the end of the long drive leading up to the house. There was a huge security gate.

'Oh, Christ. Damn,' he said.

'What's the matter?'

'My keys and card.'

'What's happened to your keys?'

'I've left them at the other place. Christ Alive. Sorry. I'm such an idiot. I need my card to get through the gate entry system.'

'Oh no. What a shame. Is there no one nearby who's got keys?'

'No. Look, why don't we go back to yours and we'll come here tomorrow. I'd love to show you around. I want this to feel like your home as well.'

Cara felt a rush of pleasure rise through her.

They returned to the car, and Tajo drove them down the hill and towards her home on the seafront.

'I'm sorry I'm so useless. Fancy forgetting my keys. It's ridiculous.'

'It doesn't matter. We'll go tomorrow,' she said, smiling warmly at him.

Cara couldn't believe how well the relationship between Taj and her had developed since she'd arrived. He stayed with her most nights and treated her with a kindness she'd never known.

'Let's stop for a drink on the way back. Let's make the most of the afternoon, given I've cocked up the plans to go to mine.'

'Don't worry. We'll go to yours another time. A drink would be lovely though.'

Tajo pulled up next to a small bar at a resort she hadn't been to before and insisted she had a rum cocktail to celebrate being in St Lucia.

'We sometimes drink rum and condensed milk, but I won't subject you to that,' he said.

'Rum and condensed milk? Really? Are you joking?'

'Nope. It's a local delicacy.'

'Well, it sounds completely disgusting.'

'Ha! All the English girls say that.'

'Oh, they do, do they? How many English girls have you offered condensed milk to, then?'

'No, I didn't mean it like that. Of course, I don't go around offering drinks to English girls. You are the only English girl for me.'

'Good job,' she said, kissing him on the cheek.

'So then, tell me all about your life at home. You've told me a little bit. Now I want to hear everything.'

Cara smiled, her fingers tracing the condensation on her glass as she began to share her story.

'Well, you know I did a degree at Birmingham University, and I'm going back in September to do a master's.'

'I do. And once you finish your master's, you will live here in St Lucia with me. You promised, remember?'

'Did I? I don't remember promising.'

'Yes, you did. We're going to be together forever. You can't have forgotten that already. Tell me about your friends...the lucky women who get to share a house with you.'

'There's Katherine, Jools, and Rachel. We're very close. We've been through so much together.'

'What are they doing now?'

'Katherine studied nursing and has started work at a hospital in Birmingham. It's a huge place, and there's lots of pressure on her, but she's loving it.'

'That's a great job to do. My mum was a nurse.'

'Was she? I thought you said she was an interior designer.'

'No. A nurse.'

'Oh, sorry - must have got confused. Where did she work?'

'No, you're telling me about you now I want to know everything. What are the other girls you live with doing?'

'Oh yes, well, there's Rachel, a budding psychiatrist. She's based at a hospital in Birmingham as well. She hoped to be at the same place as Katherine, but they are at different hospitals, which is a shame.

'The other one is Jools - she is a brilliant businesswoman. She's landed a high-flying position at HSBC business bank. She'll be worth millions in a few years.'

'She's worth millions?'

'No, I'm just saying that she will be. She's so good at all that business stuff.'

'Oh, I see. So, none of them wanted to stay on at university, like you?'

'No; it's only me who is subjecting myself to more education.'

'That's because you're more intelligent than they are.'

'Ha, ha. That's not true. I love the subject and don't feel I've finished learning all about it yet. The others are ready to get out there and get a job.'

'You don't want a job?'

'Yes, but I'm in a fortunate position; I told you about my aunty, didn't I? She left me some money. She wanted me to use it for travel and education, so I decided to stay on to do the master's degree and to travel out here for the summer. The rest of it I'll keep and use it as a deposit for a flat when I graduate. I know I'm lucky to have it.'

'Your aunt would be proud. Make sure you invest the rest of it properly. You could easily double it by the time you need it.'

'Yes, I will. I might ask you for some advice.'

'Of course. Any time.'

They sat silently for a while; the late afternoon sun was still warm, and the gentle sounds of the sea and the magical sense of being away from everything made her feel like she was in a cocoon on the other side of the world.

'Were you close to your aunt?'

'Yes, I was. She was like a mother. My parents died when I was young. She took me in and looked after me. We had our fallings out over the years, but there was no shortage of love. She'd been ill, so her death wasn't unexpected, but it was hard nevertheless. It didn't help that my boyfriend, Dean, went off with someone else at the same time. I felt like someone was holding me down and kicking me in the face...it was awful.'

'Did he know your aunt had just died?'

'Yes. He knew, but he didn't care.'

'What do you mean - he didn't care?'

'Well, it didn't stop him from finding someone new, so he can't have cared all that much. I thought he was the one; we were always so happy. He was a year above me but was doing a four-year degree, so we were together for three years and planning to move in together after graduating. I never saw any signs that anything was wrong. Out of the blue, he ended the relationship. I thought he was joking at first. There had been no signs of trouble or anything.

'In every other relationship I've had, there have been doubts and concerns, and you spend your whole time worrying about whether it will work. I thought this relationship was special because I never did any of that worrying that usually accompanies my relationships. It seemed so natural and easy. I couldn't believe it when he said he wanted to end the relationship. The bottom fell out of my world.'

'That's not on. Men shouldn't behave like that.'

'No. No one should behave like that, but unfortunately, many people do.'

'Why did the other men not sort him out?'

'How do you mean?'

'If one of my female friends were treated like that by a man, I'd go and pay him a visit.'

'You're very sweet.'

'You break a woman's heart in front of me; I'll break

you, man. I would never treat someone like that. You know I'd never behave like that with you, don't you?'

'Yes, I do.'

'You trust me, don't you?'

'Yes, of course I do.'

CHAPTER
TEN

'I'm going to get a drink; what can I get you?' said Tajo.

'I'd love a Diet Coke, thanks.'

'Lovely. I'll be back in a minute,'

Cara stretched back and enjoyed the sun warming her skin until it tingled. She felt her muscles relax for the first time after a hectic morning of scrabbling on and off windsurfers and surfboards, trying to assist children who had never done any water sports before.

After four classes, two one-on-one sessions, pulling all the equipment back to shore, and dismantling and cleaning it for the afternoon team, she was ready for a lovely rest. She closed her eyes and gently drifted off to sleep.

'So, this is where you hang out,' said a familiar voice.

She looked up to see Tom, her lovely friend from the water sports hut.

'Hello. What are you up to?'

'Nothing. Just came to see you. I wasn't sure whether you were out and about or not.

'I'm just chilling and trying to recover from this morning. That was tough, wasn't it?'

'Christ, yes. Back-to-back classes. No one's idea of fun.'

Cara could feel Tom's eyes scan across her body as they talked. He crouched beside her, absently picking at the grass beside her towel.

'So, do you have any plans this afternoon?' he asked. 'Anything exciting on the cards? If not, do you fancy lunch? Or I could put together a picnic that we could have on the beach. We could watch the other instructors working away while we drink wine.'

Cara laughed and sat up, aware of his eyes lingering on her as she adjusted her yellow bikini top. She felt an involuntary shiver travel through her, and it occurred that, as lovely, kind and caring as Tajo was, she'd never caught him looking at her like that. He'd never even tried to be inappropriate with her. She didn't know whether he found her sexy.

'Here we go,' said Tajo, returning with the diet cokes. He stood there, looking down at Tom. 'Can I help you?' he asked.

'Hi, I'm Tom. Cara's friend. We were just talking about going for a picnic on the beach.'

'You want to take my girlfriend for a picnic, do you?'

Cara reached out and touched Tajo's leg to try and calm him down.

'Look, I didn't realise she had a boyfriend. No harm done,' said Tom, backing away. 'I'll see you tomorrow, Cara.'

'Why does he want to see you tomorrow?' asked Tajo.

'I work with him. I'll be at work tomorrow. That's all he meant. Why are you so jealous.'

'I'm not jealous.'

'You were then. You looked angry when you came back.'

Tajo sat down beside her, sitting in the place recently vacated by Tom. 'Not angry one bit, my love. How are you feeling? Still aching? Shall I organise a massage for you?'

And everything was back to normal. Kind Tajo had reappeared.

'I'm fine, honestly. Perhaps you could give me a massage later?'

'I'll talk to the beauty spa and get one booked for you,' he replied. 'Make sure blond boy doesn't come back while I'm away.'

The truth was that she didn't want a massage. What she wanted was for Tajo to want to massage her. Seeing the lingering look that Tom had given her had made her think. Why did Tajo not look at her like that?

WHEN TAJO RETURNED, he was not alone.

'May I introduce Maurice?'

'Sure,' said Cara, looking up to see man beaming down at her with a soft, round face and dancing eyes.

'Lovely to meet you,' she said, running her hands through her hair. She must look a state - half asleep and greasy from copious quantities of sun cream.

'You OK?' asked Maurice.

'Yes, I'm fine,' she said. She was sitting upright now and could see him better. His face had looked angelic when she was lying down, but now it looked a little plump. His skin was terrible, with acne pitting all over his cheeks. He had a nasty-looking scar on his neck, which puckered into his chin, giving him an air of menace, which wasn't helped by the small tattoo on his cheek.

She felt immediately ill at ease. 'How do you know Tajo?'

'I've known him a long time,' he said, gently nodding his head as if moving it to an imaginary drumbeat. 'A long, long time.'

'OK. So, do you work together?'

'Sometimes,' he said, resuming the head nodding. 'Sometimes we do, sometimes we don't.'

Cara decided she didn't like him one bit.

LATER THAT DAY, as Cara and Tajo sat drinking wine after a small lunch, listening to the sounds of the sea through the open windows; she turned to him. 'Your friend Maurice. How did he get that scar on his neck?'

'Probably fighting.'

'Fighting?'

'I don't know. He probably got in trouble with some troublemakers.'

'Have you never asked him? I'm surprised you don't know...'

'No, I never even thought to ask him. I'll find out for you if you like.'

'No, don't do that; I thought it looked nasty. I wondered what had happened.'

'We used to get into a lot of trouble when we were younger. Always joshing around and causing problems. I assumed he was injured in a fight somewhere. A lot of people carry knives on the island, you know. It can be a dangerous place at night. When I was young, I was in a lot of trouble. It's difficult growing up without a mother and father.'

'I thought you had your mum? Didn't you say she was a nurse?'

'No. She died when I was a baby.'

'You definitely said she was a nurse, I'm sure of it.'

'Sorry to confuse you, angel. No – I was just saying how dangerous it can be on the island.'

'Do you think it's dangerous here in Lobster Bay?'

'No, it's very safe here. But it can get quite difficult in Castres and places on the other side of the island. But you don't have to worry about that because I'll always be here to protect you.'

'Thank you. I haven't felt unsafe in all the time I've been here. I'm loving my time in St Lucia.'

'I'm glad. I'd like you to meet more of my friends. They are nice. You'll like them a lot.'

'Sure,' she said, silently hoping they weren't as dodgy looking as Maurice.

'How about tomorrow night? I have a friend with a magnificent boat which is moored in Marigot Bay – do you remember me mentioning them before? There's a group of people gathering there for drinks. Shall I tell them we'll join them? We could go there for the evening, then go to my place afterwards for cocktails and swimming in the pool.'

'I'd love that. A party on a boat sounds terribly posh. Are they very wealthy?'

'They weren't. I mean - they are successful, but not hugely wealthy, then they invested in the Lajan fund and made millions, so one of them bought a boat.'

'Really? They made that much money?'

'Yes. Financial investment is straightforward. Everyone thinks it's so complicated, but it isn't. The experts want you to think it's difficult, so they keep their jobs.'

'Ha. Ha. I'm sure you're right. Do you think I should use my money to make more money?'

'I'm sure you've got your money invested somewhere already. Leave it where it is.'

'To be honest, it's just in the bank.'

'Oh no. That's no good. Have you had a financial adviser look at the whole thing for you? It might be worth talking to someone who knows about these things.'

'I should have done that before coming away, shouldn't I?'

'Don't worry. It sounds like you had enough to worry about after losing your aunt and then your boyfriend. You can sort it all out now - but don't go headlong into anything. Talk to an expert before doing a thing. I know a very good financial adviser here. I can get him to pop over and talk to you?'

'Could you? That would be great. Thanks.'

Taj picked up his phone and sent what seemed like a barrage of texts.

'He'll be here in an hour. I have to finish some work now, but I'll see you tomorrow for the boat party, OK?'

'Brilliant,' she said, lying back on the sunbed to catch the reminder of the sun's rays.

Cara awoke and looked at her watch; the financial guy would arrive in 20 minutes. She rushed into the small hut to spruce herself up a little bit. She wasn't used to talking to financial advisors, and she was sure they would expect far more from a woman with six-figure sums in her bank. She was wearing board shorts and a t-shirt and was still smelling of the sea.

Minutes later, she re-emerged, carrying a deckchair and placing it beside hers. She had borrowed a picnic table, which she put in front of the chairs to make it as business-like as possible. She hoped he wasn't surprised or put off by how amateurish it all was.

If the financial advisor was surprised by the way she looked, she was incredibly surprised at him. She saw him coming across the grass, dressed in a suit designed for a man twice his size—it was comically large. He looked like a little boy starting school in an oversized uniform because his mum didn't want him to grow out of it by the end of term.

He wore little, round glasses that reminded her of Harry Potter as he trundled along, looking hot and bothered as he adjusted the tie that he was clearly unused to wearing.

'Cara?' he asked.

'Yes, that's me,' she said. He was a small man with very dark skin and eyes like coal.

He greeted her warmly and laid a briefcase on the table, it looked at it as if it had come tumbling out of the 1970s.

'I didn't catch your name,' said Cara.

'Jesus,' he said.

'Oh right, OK. Nice to meet you, Jesus. You look very smart.'

'Thank you. I always wear made-to-measure designer clothes.'

It was one of those occasions on which Cara wished her friends back home could be there. If the suit was made to measure, then Jesus had clearly given the tailor the wrong measurements. She smiled at him, he smiled at her, and opened the briefcase infront of them, pulling out a notebook.

'So, my name is Jesus. I am from the Financial Services St Lucia office. Here's my card,' he said, offering a rather smart card with the company logo printed on the front, a swirl of colours with FSSL embossed in gold. 'I am in charge of new business, and Tajo said you needed advice.'

'Yes, I think so.'

'Well, we are St Lucia's leading financial services providers. We used to be part of the Bank of St Lucia, but now we are an independent arm, helping high-net-worth individuals. If there's anything I can help with, do say.'

Cara decided that she liked him. Her initial views of his appearance had been replaced by an appreciation of his calm nature and unpushy manner. She began explaining about her money which was in a normal savings account.

'Ah, no. That's not a good idea. Unless your money works for you, having it has little point.'

'Sure. I wanted to put it somewhere safe until I'm ready to buy a home...I'll need it as a deposit, and I don't want to take any risks with it.'

'Most investments carry risks, but I know of one that is a great option. Few risks and large returns. Would you like to hear about it? It's called the Lajan Investment Fund.'

'Oh, I know all about it. Tajo told me. How can I get involved in that? Can I invest straight away? Maybe just put £1000 in?'

'Of course you can,' said Jesus, adjusting his tie and reaching back into his case. 'I'll prepare everything now.'

CHAPTER
ELEVEN

The aroma of grilled fish and spicy Caribbean flavours wafted through the air as Cara and her colleagues gathered for lunch. Blankets had been laid out on the sand, and a large barbecue sizzled away while gentle reggae sounds danced in the air.

'So, what's the occasion for this fancy lunch? I'm not complaining, but it seems a bit much for a regular workday.'

'I thought you knew. We're celebrating a very special birthday today.'

Cara's eyes widened. 'Really? Whose birthday is it?'

'It's Tom's,' Pete revealed, clapping Tom on the back. 'The big 25, can you believe it?'

Cara turned to Tom, her mouth agape. 'Why didn't you tell me it was your birthday?'

Tom shrugged, a sheepish grin on his face. 'I didn't want to make a big deal out of it.'

Cara shook her head, a smile tugging at the corners of her lips. 'Well, happy birthday, old man. You're officially over the hill now.'

Tom clutched his chest in mock offence. 'Ouch, Cara. Way to make a guy feel special on his big day. Are you coming out with us tonight to celebrate? We're going to Rum Bar - the one on the seafront. It's only about 10 minutes away.'

'Oh, I'd love to, but I've made plans with Tajo. I'm going to a party on a boat with him. Maybe if I look out from the boat, I'll be able to see you all at the bar.'

'Sure. Yes. You have plans. Of course.'

Tom's disappointment was evident in his tone, his smile faltering slightly. Cara felt a twinge of guilt. She'd been working there for three weeks and had got to know the guys well. She'd have liked to party with them, but she'd already made plans with Tajo; she couldn't change them now.

'I'm sorry. I didn't realise it was your birthday. A boat party sounds fun, though, doesn't it? I'll tell you all about it tomorrow.'

'Sure,' said Tom. 'So, you and Tajo are the real deal, are you? I wasn't sure when I bumped into you.'

Cara shifted uncomfortably. 'Yeah, we've been seeing each other for a while now. I met him the day I arrived.

Tom leaned back, his expression thoughtful. 'I know it's none of my business, but when I saw you both the other day, he seemed quite aggressive. Is he always like that?'

Cara waved off his concern, forcing a smile. 'Oh, he just gets a little jealous sometimes. He's nice once you get to know him.'

Cara's mind drifted to Tajo's intense gaze and possessive touch. She knew he could be overwhelming sometimes, but it was just his way of showing affection.

Tom didn't look convinced, but he let the subject drop. 'Well, if you change your mind, you know where to find us.

And if you ever need anything, you know I'm here for you, right?'

Cara smiled, touched by his concern. 'I know, Tom. Thank you.'

As the conversation shifted to other topics, Cara found herself lost in thought. She knew Tajo could be a bit intense sometimes, but he was passionate, that was all. And sure, maybe he got a little jealous now and then, but that just meant he cared about her. Anyway, she was determined to enjoy the excitement of the boat party and the promise of the investment scheme.

∿

It was 5 p.m., and Cara's phone was wedged against the dressing table mirror in her tiny hut. She chatted to her friends on loudspeaker while unpacking the contents of her wardrobe onto her bed.

'I've got nothing to wear.'

'Yes, you have,' said Katherine. 'Stop panicking. It's most unlikely for you to worry about clothes. And I'm sure he won't judge you if he is as lovely as you say.'

'I know, it's just that I want to make a good impression. I've never met these friends before, and we're going on this amazing boat trip. I don't want to be the only one not dressed nicely.'

'Don't be silly; you always look absolutely lovely,' said Jools. 'What about that red dress? That looks good on you.'

'I don't think I brought it with me,' said Cara, picking up and throwing clothing around. 'I guess I thought I wouldn't need anything dressy. I wish I had time to go to the shops or something. Although I don't want to spend anything, I want to invest everything. Did I tell you I saw a financial adviser who told me about this amazing scheme - called Lajan. I've started investing in it. Only a small amount, but it's amazing. I've made money already.'

She picked up a green dress but thought better of it, casting it aside and pulling open drawers. 'I've got no nice shoes and didn't have time to go to the hairdressers. Oh, hang on - is this the blue dress you mentioned, Jools? That's quite nice.'

She pulled out a scrunched-up dress in desperate need of a good iron. It was in a beautiful sky blue that would work well with her new tan and was perfectly suitable for a party on a boat.

'Rewind a bit,' said Katherine. 'What did you say about the financial adviser? He told you to invest the money that your auntie gave you in his scheme?'

'It's not his scheme. It's a very successful scheme here in St Lucia. I saw him yesterday and I put £1k into it. That's all.'

'Oh God - be careful.'

'I am careful. I'm taking advice.'

'I know, but some of those investments are a complete scam.'

'Not this one. My £1000 is now worth £1200. OVERNIGHT. Tajo has invested a lot of money and made a tonne of cash.'

'Tajo is the guy you've been seeing?'

'Yes. He advised me to talk to a financial adviser first.'

'Oh right, I guess that's okay then. How did you find a financial adviser out there?'

'Through Tajo.'

'Shouldn't you go to a proper, independent financial adviser? I know it might cost something, but you need independent advice,' said Jools.

'He was independent. Anyway, they do things differently here. All I care about is that it's a really good investment, and I'm really happy, and I know my aunty would approve of me making as much of it as I can; it just means I can do more things if I have more money. That's all she ever wanted for me. Now, this dress, what do you think?'

'It will need a bloody good iron,' said Rachel, peering at the screen to see the dress that Cara was valiantly holding up.

'Yes, I know; I need to borrow an iron. Look, it's lovely to talk to you. I'll try and take some pictures on the boat tonight. I love you all.'

∽

IN A SMALL FLAT IN BIRMINGHAM, three friends looked from one to another.

'Are you as worried as I am?' asked Jools.

'Yep. What the hell is she doing, investing her money in some madcap scheme.'

'She spoke to a financial adviser. Perhaps it will all work out?' she Rachel.

'Yeah, maybe,' said Jools. 'I hope so.'

∽

'OH, MY GOD.'

Cara stared disbelievingly at the beautiful white boat with OMEROS embossed in gold writing across the side. 'Are we going on this?'

'We certainly are, beautiful.'

'My God. You know that Omeros was Derek Walcott's seminal work, don't you?'

'I do. I also know it's divided into seven books, and there are seven cabins on the boat to reflect this.'

They had travelled to the large, elegant yacht in a small motorboat. It was only a 20-minute walk around the coast from the hotel, but arriving by sea made the whole thing so much more glamorous. Cara had never seen anything quite like the boat. It looked as if it belonged to Hollywood royalty.

'What do your friends who own this do?' said Cara, holding onto Tajo's arm. 'I don't think they'll be very impressed with me and my little windsurfing classes.'

'Of course they will. They manage business portfolios and have made most of their money through the same scheme you have started to invest in, so they are certainly no better than you. And you are much, much prettier.'

Tajo draped his arm around her shoulders, and she cuddled closely into him as the summer sun warmed her face. She could think of nowhere on earth she'd rather be.

'Have you checked on the portfolio recently?'

'Yes,' she said. 'It's grown. I can't believe it.'

'It's great, isn't it? I've never known anything like it.

My investment has grown more than any other investment I've ever made. I am going to put loads of money into it tomorrow.'

'Do you think I should do the same?' she asked.

'It's up to you. You might want to take financial advice first, just to be sure, but from my point of view, it's a good way to make easy money. If your money is just sitting in a savings account, you are much better off putting it into an investment like this; you could double your investment, then take out everything you put in and still have £100,000 in there. But don't do anything without checking with the experts first. Or chat to some of the guys on the boat - they know all about it.'

She kissed him gently on the side of his cheek. So, this was how people made money. You certainly needed money to make money.

As their small boat approached the yacht, four smartly dressed crew members appeared on deck to help them on board. 'Welcome,' said a cheery woman with sparkling teeth, dressed in a white uniform. She sounded American. 'Have a glass of champagne and Kriselle will take you onto the main deck aft where the other guests are assembled.'

They walked across the boat's main salon, through a beautiful bar and up some steps. On board, it was as gorgeous as it had looked from the outside. Immaculate walnut interior, white linen on soft day beds and beautiful bowls of fresh lilies everywhere. It smelled new, of freshly polished wood, leather and money. Yep - more than anything, it smelled of money.

Cara wondered what these people would be like. She hoped against hope that they were kind and friendly like Tajo. If they were snotty, middle-aged bankers with ruddy complexions and fat stomachs, talking about their 'clubs' and how much they enjoyed 'rugger,' she might throw herself overboard.

'Your hosts are just through here,' said the steward, leading them past a gorgeous jacuzzi towards a bar and seating area at the back of the boat.

'Thank you,' said Cara, feeling a whirl of butterfly wings inside her. They turned the corner, and she saw a group of people sitting there. They weren't Tajo's friends, surely - these were very rough-looking men, with a handful of women dressed as if they were going to the opera in Milan, dripping with earrings, perfume and make-up. Fingernails like spears, necklaces and earrings weighed down with heavy diamonds.

Who were these people? They looked completely out of place on this luxury yacht.

'Hey, how you doing, man?' said Tajo, stepping into the throng and doing that macho hug where men clasp hands at chest level as if they're about to do a hand wrestle and drop their shoulders in towards one another.

'Come and join us. Bring the pretty lady,' said a guy with half his eyebrow shaved off and replaced with a faded tattoo that could no longer be read. 'You come to join the black folk today, have you?'

Cara smiled. 'Certainly looks that way,' she said nervously. These really weren't what she was expecting at all. She certainly needn't have worried about them being over-fed boarding school types.

'My name's Rok Chuckles,' said the guy who appeared to be the alpha male in the throng. Never has a name been so inappropriate. He didn't look as if he'd ever chuckled in his life. She leaned in to shake his hand, and he pulled her close. She noticed an ugly scar running down the side of his face. His eyes were cold and dark. They made her feel instantly wary. He had a yellow bandana hanging out of his top pocket, a large ring with an enormous yellow jewel on his little finger, and a lion tattoo roaring up the side of his face.

'Come on, you,' said Tajo, sweeping in to rescue her and introduce her to the rest of the group. Sadly, none of them were any more likeable. She wasn't a snob by any means, and Tajo himself wasn't erudite or literary, but these guys were something else. They all looked slightly dirty and very dangerous. 'Your girl looks scared,' said Chuckles. 'Tell her I'm a nice guy, you know.'

'She knows that. Give her a break. She's meeting you all for the first time.'

'I'm a softy,' said Chuckles. 'Soft right through. Come meet the ladies, Cara. This is Theresa, and this is Venna.' She noticed him slap Venna's bottom as he made the introductions. 'Now, are you ready for another drink?'

'Yes, a mojito would be lovely, thanks. If that's OK?'

'Hey, anything is OK for you, my love. I'll get you the best mojito you have ever tasted.'

Cara watched him click his fingers and signal to a waiter. Christ, he was rude. She decided to head off to find the loos while rum, mint, and limes were shaken, stirred, and poured. She walked out of the bar area and remembered her promise to send photos back to the girls, so she turned to take a couple of shots of the group.

Then she continued her journey to find the toilets, which turned out to be nestled in the corner of the boat, with portholes for windows and nautical toilet paper.

From the comfort of the toilet cubicle, Cara sent the pictures to the house WhatsApp group so Rachel, Katherine and Jools could enjoy the splendour of the boat.

'Wow, wow, wow. That is like something from a dream. MY GOD!' wrote Rachel.

'Which one is Tajo?' Jools replied.

'Third man from the left.'

'Who are all those other guys? His friends?' wrote Rachel.

Before Cara could answer, she heard the door to the toilets open and heavy footsteps.

'Cara, are you in there?' said a female voice.

'Yes.'

'OK, just checking. Is everything OK?'

'Yes, of course. Who is that?'

'It's Theresa. You met me by the bar.'

'Oh, yes. I won't be long.'

'No rush.'

Cara put her phone away, opened the cubicle door, and came out to see Theresa and Venna standing there.

'Hi,' she said.

'Hi, look - I hope you don't mind us asking this, but the boat's owner is a very private man. He doesn't like photos of the boat to be taken.'

'Oh, I'm so sorry. I just took a few of the group as I left and some of the boat's interior.'

'Yes. We need to ask you to delete them.'

'Delete them?'

'Yes.'

'Sure, OK. I'll delete them.'

Cara moved to the sink and attempted to switch on the tap. It was one of those new-fangled ones where you can't figure out whether to touch, turn, or put your hands underneath it.

'Perhaps I could delete them for you while you wash your hands?'

'It's fine. I'll do it in a minute,' said Cara, flapping her hands around to get the water out.

Venna leaned over and pushed the sides of the tap, the only movement that Cara hadn't tried. Water cascaded out.

'We'd like you to delete the pictures before leaving the bathroom,' said Venna.

'Yes, OK.' Cara pulled out her phone, and the two women looked over her shoulder as she deleted them one-by-one.

'Thank you,' said Theresa, opening the door for her. Cara headed back to Tajo feeling miserable and out of sorts. Where the hell was she? Who were these people not letting her take photos? She looked around at them all - pimped out in designer gear and dripping in gold. How could her lovely boyfriend be friends with these people? She knocked back a mojito and ordered another. It took a lot to make her feel like this, but - for God's sake - they'd made money through an investment plan - that was all that separated her from them. They weren't all that special.

She thought of Tom partying at Rum Bar. They'd probably be dancing on the beach by now. She really should have gone out with them instead.

'Are you OK?' Tajo asked her, gently kissing the top of her head. 'You've gone all quiet.'

'Yeah. I feel a bit odd here. I don't think I fit in.'

'Of course you do. Once you get to know them, you'll think they're great.' Tajo signalled to a very tall man with rangy arms and legs like a giraffe. 'Come and meet Cara. She's one of us...an investor in the Lajan Scheme.' 'Charmed I'm sure,' he said in a strong Jamaican accent, bowing slightly as he took her hand. 'Have you made a fortune? I've bought a house. So much money.'

'I haven't invested much yet. Not quite enough to buy a house.'

'Ah, well, I hope it keeps growing for you. You can just add or take money out whenever you want,' he said. 'No need to do it til you feel comfortable.'

'Thank you. Yes, I know how to do that,' said Cara.

As they talked, Chuckles walked over to them and pushed his way into the group.

'How are you enjoying the boat?' he asked.

'It's beautiful,' she replied.

'You're part of the gang now. Let me know if I can do anything for you at any stage. I'm quite good at sorting things out.'

He handed her a business card.

'Thank you,' she said, but she couldn't imagine any scenario on earth in which she'd be summoning his help.

'I mean that – any friend of Tajo's is a friend of ours. If you need anything done, you call me on that number, and I'll help.'

'That's very kind,' she said. He made her feel slightly nervous; she didn't know why; it was almost like she was in a scene from a mafia film where the head of the family was offering to kill people for you.

'One day you will have a beautiful boat like this,' he said.

'Wow, I don't think I could ever afford anything like this. It's absolutely beautiful.'

'But your investment's working out, isn't it? That's all gone well for you?'

'Yes, it's been amazing.'

That's how I bought this boat, investing like you have. I put everything into the scheme and watched the money double and triple. Then, I took out my initial stake. You can't lose. You should invest a bit more; the bigger the stake, the bigger the prize.'

'Yes, I'm just worried about losing any of the money. I feel comfortable with what I've invested.'

'Sure, you need to do what you feel comfortable with, but this is a once-in-a-lifetime opportunity; I'm putting everything I've got into this, and - as friendly advice - I would if I were you.'

A new glass of mojito sat before her. She took a large gulp. The women who'd accosted her in the toilets stared at her as she drank. She was still cross with them and glared back until they looked away. 'Are those women involved in the investment plan? I don't like them at all.'

Alcohol was making her unusually candid.

'No, of course not. Just a chosen few are involved, or the whole thing would become overwhelmed, and returns would drop.'

She loved the idea of making a fortune in investments... of being more than an academic. She wanted to show these horrible women what she was made of. She'd have a boat like this one day, with all her lovely friends on it, and they would sail past these women in a dinghy.

'I'd like to invest all my money,' she said.

How often did you come across an investment with a guaranteed 40 to 50% return? Why would she not put every penny she had into it?

'I'll do it now.'

The steward poured her a couple more drinks, and she wandered up to the deck, enjoying the freshness of the night air. She checked her account. The money had been transferred. She had just invested every last penny she had into the Lajan Scheme, seduced by the promise of easy money and the desire to prove herself to these wealthy strangers. The alcohol buzzed through her veins, dulling the nagging doubts that tugged at the edges of her consciousness.

The salty sea breeze whipped through her hair as she stood on the deck, the yacht cutting through the inky black waters. The moon hung low in the sky, casting an eerie glow on the ocean's surface. Cara's heart pounded in her chest, a mixture of excitement and trepidation coursing through her body.

She thought back to Tom's concerned words, his gentle warning about Tajo's aggressive behaviour. She thought of her friends back home, their worried faces on the phone screen as she told them about the investment scheme. But most of all, she thought of the money, the tantalising possibility of wealth beyond her wildest dreams.

With a deep breath, Cara turned back towards the party, her eyes glittering with a newfound determination. She would see this through, no matter the cost. She had to believe that the Lajan Scheme was her ticket to a better life, her chance to prove to everyone - including herself - that she was destined for greatness.

But as she rejoined the group, her smile plastered firmly in place, Cara couldn't escape the cold, creeping sensation that she had just made the biggest mistake of her life.

\>

CHAPTER
TWELVE

Mary's story: Saturday 6th July
TWO WEEKS LATER

'So, we're sure about this, are we?'

'Yes. Come on, let's not overthink it. We'll head down to the boat where the party is taking place and ask for Cara Jeffries.'

'And what then?' asks Ted. 'Just hand her the purse?'

'No, we'll take her aside and ask whether she's lost anything.'

'Then give her the purse?'

'I guess. It's her purse, after all.'

'I think we should take all the money, the map, and the key out of it. Then, we can hand over the purse publicly and ask her to meet us somewhere in private to get the money. She won't want it waved around on a boat in front of everyone on the boat.'

'OK, yes - that sounds sensible.'

'Finally, we agree on something,' says Ted, nudging me affectionately.

∼

It's 7 p.m. when we leave our chalet and walk towards reception. I swear to God—my excitement is off the scale. Butterflies dance in my stomach, and I keep biting my cheek to calm myself.

We have decided to get a cab from reception, even though we'd both prefer to leave the hotel without the staff being aware of our departure. But we know how difficult it will be to get a cab when we're out on the road, and we're not sure how safe it is to wander around flagging down cars when we've got thousands of pounds stuffed in Ted's pocket, so we're biting the bullet and getting one from the hotel.

We arrive at reception to see Amelia standing there. She looks as beautiful as always but not as well put together as earlier. She looks like a woman who has been rushing around all day.

'I'm so sorry about this morning. I hope those police officers didn't disturb you too much. I spoke to them afterwards and said they must phone first if they need anything else. I'm very sorry if they interrupted your day.'

'Not at all,' says Ted. 'Please don't worry. Everything was fine.'

'Oh good. Is there anything I can help you with?'

'Yes, please. We're here to get the cab we ordered earlier...over to Marigold Bay.'

'Yes, of course. It's at the front of the hotel. Royalty will show you.'

Royalty emerges from behind a door as if he always

hovers there, poised and awaiting instruction. He smiles engagingly before leading us to a rusty Toyota. As he pulls the door open, I think it will come off its hinges. It's so funny to see a well-dressed butler opening the door of a rust heap of a car for us, so I take a quick picture before Royalty checks that we're seated, then doffs his cap flamboyantly and twirls it in the air as he sinks into a dramatic bow.

'Oh, look at that,' I say to Ted. 'You should do that whenever I leave the room.'

'Yeah,' he says, touching his jacket pocket. His fingers drum a nervous rhythm against the fabric, constantly checking that the money is secure. I have the purse in my handbag.

This. Is. So. Exciting.

We arrive in Marigot Bay and step out of the taxi. The place is blindingly beautiful, like Cannes in those films from the 60s, full of beautiful people, perfect seas and shops and restaurants twinkling in the fading light. The place is a crescent-shaped cove hugged by emerald hillsides. Of course, there are the beautiful turquoise waters, I'm starting to get used to those now. But these turquoise waters lap at a marina with luxury yachts and colourful fishing boats. Palms sway lazily in the gentle breeze, their fronds casting dappled shadows over the sandy beach. It's beautiful. I have to get photos of it all.

There are tenders tied up at the side, each sporting the names of the boats they are transporting passengers out to. We look for Omeros and tell the driver we have been invited to a party.

'Step aboard,' he says, helping me to clamber onto the boat while keeping my dignity intact. Ted has gone quiet, as always when he feels under pressure, so I take pictures of the amazing scenery and the fabulous seafront we are leaving behind. I also chat away like I'm on drugs. Occasionally, I peer into my bag to check the black purse is still there.

The gentle rocking of the tender has a soothing effect. The warm Caribbean breeze, the scent of salt air mingled with the sweetness of tropical blooms, the sounds of gently lapping waves and chattering seabirds—it's wonderful.

'Mr and Mrs, We are here,' says our driver, lifting his cap. Ted tips him, and we step off and onto a magnificent boat.

'Come in, please - have a glass of champagne,' says a smartly dressed woman in nautical colours. I reach out to take one, but Ted stops me. 'Let's not drink here,' he says.

'Why?' I mean - I know we can't get drunk at a party we haven't been invited to, but one glass of champagne? Surely that's OK.

'Look around,' he says.

That's when I glance into the boat and realise two things:

1. Everyone is staring at us.

2. It looks like we've stepped onto a crime drama set. Muscled men in tight-fitting suits stare back at us. I see tattoos, scars and angry eyes.

3. There appear to be no women on the boat. Where are the women?

~

'WHAT YA DOIN'?' asks a man who looks like he knows his way around a boxing ring. He has a yellow bandana tied around his wrist, a large ring with an enormous yellow jewel on his little finger, and a tattoo on his face that looks like a lion, a tiger, or something. His gruff voice sends a chill down my spine, and I instinctively step closer to Ted.

'This is private property.'

'Yes, of course,' says Ted, trying to sound jolly and unflustered. 'Sorry to just step aboard like this. I'm Ted. This is Mary.'

The man stares through Ted. He doesn't comment. People gather behind the yellow bandana man, and the sound of voices, music, and clinking glasses comes from further back in the boat.

'Look, we're sorry to turn up unannounced. We just wanted to talk to someone at the party.'

'Who?' asks the man.

'Cara Jeffries,' says Ted.

Suddenly, everything goes quiet. The air grows thick with tension, and I can feel the weight of their gazes pressing down on us.

'Who?' asks the man.

'Cara Jeffrfies,' repeats Ted.

'Is this some sort of fucking joke?'

Everyone is staring at them. There's a feeling of real danger. My heart pounds in my chest, and I fight the urge to turn and run. Who the hell is Cara Jeffries?

'It's not a joke at all. We were led to believe she would be on this boat.'

The men continue to stare.

'Look, if she's not here, that's fine. We found her purse on the beach and it had an invitation to this party, so we thought we'd come and return the purse.'

'How could it have an invitation to this party? This is a private party, and it was only arranged yesterday. Cara went missing days ago.'

'I don't know,' says Ted, cautiously.

'Yes, you do,' says the man. 'You know where she is, don't you?'

'I don't know anything. Why are you all so aggressive? I've just come to see Cara.'

The staring continues. I can't keep quiet any longer.

'Look, is she here or not? We don't understand what the problem is. We found this purse, and we're trying to return it to her.'

'And you found it on the beach?'

'Yes.'

'Was it you who dug up the beach?'

'No, of course not.'

'You don't know what you're getting yourselves involved in here. But, I swear to God, you tell us if you know where she is. He looks me up and down aggressively, pausing as his eyes reach my breasts. He jabs his finger at me as he speaks. 'You know what's going on, don't you? You're a friend of hers. Have you been hiding her? The woman's gone missing, and you turn up here asking for her and saying you found a purse. What are you talking about?'

'We don't know who she is or where she is.' Ted steps towards the scar-faced hooligan and I feel my heart leap into my mouth. Surely, to God, he can see how dangerous these people are.

'We are trying to do the right thing. Do not jab your finger at my wife like that, or you and I are going to have serious problems.'

Shit. We're dead.

There's a short pause, then he takes a step backwards and apologises, impressed with Ted's chivalrous behaviour.

'Looking after your woman. Good man,' he says. 'Now give me the purse.'

Ted just stares at him.

'The purse.'

I rummage inside my bag and pull out the empty purse. I hand it over with the party invitation with her name on it. My hands tremble slightly as I pass it to him, and I pray he doesn't notice.

'We're leaving now,' says Ted, stepping to one side to help me back onto the tender. 'I hope you manage to sort out the problem here.'

'Let's go,' says Ted to the tender driver. But the driver is staring up at the man on the boat. His face is ashen, eyes wide with fear. 'We need to go now,' repeats Ted with more than a hint of fear in his voice.

The tender driver jumps into action, starts the boat up and whizzes us back to shore. I take a sneaky glance behind to see them all watching us depart. The weight of their stares follows us across the water, and I don't breathe easily until we're back on solid ground.

∽

'You were so brave tonight. I was terrified, but you were having none of it,' I tell Ted when we are back in our room. He keeps staring into space and cracking his knuckles. I've never seen him like this, his usual calm demeanour replaced by restless energy.

'Do you want to talk about it?' I ask.

'I'm fine,' he says, putting his arm around me and pulling me close. 'Absolutely fine.'

I snuggle up to him, and we sit there, each enjoying our own thoughts, until Ted breaks the silence.

'That man was rude. He was a bully. Surrounded by all his thug gang and prodding his finger at you. Who does he think he is?' he says.

'I know. He was horrible. They all were.'

'Scumbags.'

'What do you think the issue is with this Cara Jeffries? They don't like her at all.'

'No, they don't. And we're going to find out exactly why.'

'We are?'

'Yes, I'm angry now. We're going to the station tomorrow morning to find out what the key is and work out what's happening. They have made me cross. Dickheads.'

'OK,' I say.

'I'm not scared of those scumbags.'

'Maybe we should be a little bit scared of them?'

'No, not at all. We're going to find out exactly what's going on.'

WE ARE SNUGGLED UP in bed that night when Ted leans over and takes my phone. 'Come on. Let's cheer ourselves up and look at today's photos, shall we?'

'Oh yes. Let's.'

He opens the photo app on my phone and scans through them. There's the picture of the rusty bucket of a taxi and some terrible photos from the car. That never works, does it? I'm always trying to take pictures through car windows; all you get is a blurry mess of colours.

'Here we are,' he says, pulling up a lovely picture of Marigot Bay. It's a beautiful shot.

'It's a shame that car's there, isn't it? That's a gorgeous picture. Can you remove the pickup truck from it?'

'Yeah, I'll get someone at work to do it. I've no idea how to do it myself.'

There are beautiful shots around Rodney Bay and a few of the boat.

'That's one impressive-looking beast,' says Ted. 'I wonder how on earth they afforded that.'

'Obviously criminals,' I say.

'Yeh. They were so rough, weren't they?'

Then we get to the photos of the bay as we come in on the tender. They are even more beautiful than the ones we took on the way out. The bay has taken on a warm, golden glow, reflecting off the calm waters. The colours are so vivid, so otherworldly that, for a moment, I forget to breathe.

'Oh, these are great. You should enter them into a photographic contest,' I say.

Then I notice it.

'Can you believe this?' I say. 'There's another damn pickup truck in the background ruining another perfect shot.'

'Don't worry, angel. I'll get someone to remove them.'

'And this picture... Hang on...'

'What is it?'

'It's the same pickup. Look, you can see the number plate here. How would that pickup get into all our shots?'

Ted sits up and takes the phone off me. His brow furrows as he studies the images, a sense of unease settling over us.

'Unless it was following us?' he says. He flicks back through the pictures. We spot six separate sightings of the car.

'We need to know who this belongs to,' says Ted, getting out of bed to fetch a paper and pen. He writes down the registration number PA1988.

'How are we going to find out who owns it?' I ask.

'No idea. I'll try googling it.'

'Will the owner's name come up?'

'I don't know. Let's have a look.'

While Ted clicks away on his phone, sighing as he tries to identify the owner, I pull up the pictures on my phone and attempt to focus on the vehicle. I check the registration number Ted wrote down...yes, that's right. There appear to be no identifying marks on the pickup itself. I flick through some more frames until I come to a picture of the vehicle front. I zoom in so much that the picture is all blurred, then gently zoom back out again.

'Oh My God,' I say to Ted.

'What is it? What's the matter?'

'I know whose car it is.'

I hand the phone to Ted and he peers at the picture before him. He sees the 'I love Darren Sammy' sticker on the windscreen. Recognition dawns on his face, quickly replaced by a look of disbelief.

'It's Happy's car.'

'I know.'

'Why is Happy following us?'

CHAPTER THIRTEEN

Mary's story: 7th July

I'VE WOKEN up in a terrible temper. I'm not sure whether it's the fact that we were confronted by an array of criminals last night, that our little mate Happy followed us, or that Ted is snoring and breathing very heavily in a thoroughly annoying fashion. Or perhaps it's all three; I'm not sure.

I decide to wake Ted up out of pure spite. 'Morning,' I say, leaning into him with an aggressive nudge. His eyes open and stay open. He's staring, unblinking, at the ceiling. The whites of his eyes are tinged with red, betraying the restless night we both endured.

'Everything OK?' he asks.

'Yes, fine. Did you sleep well?'

'I got up a couple of times to pace the room in a manly fashion, but - besides that - yes, not bad.'

I smile at him and kiss him gently on the cheek.

'I should have gone there on my own last night. It makes me sick to think of the danger I put you in.'

'I wanted to go,' I say. 'You didn't put me in danger. I put myself in danger.'

'The guy with the ridiculous scar wagging his fingers at you like that. What an absolute knob.'

'Yeah, but besides the danger element, it was a good trip, wasn't it?'

'Yeah. I guess if you ignore the fact that they could have murdered us, it was a great trip.'

'I can't get over the fact that Happy was following us. That's odd.'

'Yep, very odd. I don't know what that was about.'

'Either he was looking out for us, so why didn't he stop us before we jumped aboard the tender? Or, he's part of that group of dodgy men, and, for some reason, he is also interested in Cara Jeffries's whereabouts.'

'We'll see him this morning, won't we? It'll be interesting to see what he says.'

'Will we see him this morning?'

'Yes. On the trip.'

Oh God. I'd forgotten about that. We are booked onto a morning trip to an old church in the mountainside near Castries, the capital. It sounded like a gorgeous thing to do when we were sitting in the cold in England, looking through all the brochures and admiring the sights of the sunshine bouncing off the hillside: the flowers, the birds, the majesty of the old church.

Now, though - it's the last thing I want to do. The idea of venturing out into the unknown with Happy as our guide fills me with a sense of unease that I can't quite shake.

'After everything that happened last night, I'm sure we can give the trip a miss, can't we?'

'I think we should go on it,' says Ted. 'Happy is leading this trip, and I want to look him in the eye and see whether he quivers under the pressure of my gaze.'

'Quivers under your gaze? Are we in some sort of Western or something? This town ain't big enough for the both of us.'

'Ha, ha. There won't be pistols at dawn, but last night was odd. Whichever way you look at it. We shouldn't do anything to rouse suspicion. If we cancel the trip, it will raise concerns in his mind.'

'What will we do with the money while we're out?'

'I think we'll have to take it. I'll go straight from the tour to the train station and see what's in the locker. But only if I can do it without it looking suspicious. Then I can see you back here.'

'What do you mean you'll see me back here? What are you talking about? I'm coming with you.'

'No, I don't think that's a good idea.'

'Yes, it is. It's a very bad idea for you to go alone.'

'I don't want you in any danger.'

'And I don't want you in any danger.'

'I think it will be much easier if I do this alone.'

'For God's sake, Ted. We're married - we do these things together.'

Ted has a look of exasperation on his face as he looks at me and shakes his head.

'It's my job to protect you,' he says.

'Nope. It's our job to protect each other. We're going together, and that's final. And I don't think we should go on this trip this morning.'

'We're going,' he replies. His tone brokers no argument, and I know that any further protests will fall on deaf ears.

The godforsaken trip leaves at 8 am, of course. It

couldn't leave at a sensible time of day, could it? I get dressed like a recalcitrant toddler and follow Ted through the door.

'You're going to love this,' says Ted, packing a sports bag with suntan lotion, water, and some crackers and nuts that are sitting in a basket on the fridge. It's like we are about to go on some long-distance military expedition. I force myself not to comment.

We walk to the front of the hotel and see Happy standing in the carpark. He waves like a lunatic.

'Hey, Blondie. Give us a smile.'

He is next to the pickup that followed us to the boat last night. It's very creepy to think of him stalking us like that, but I smile sweetly and wave back.

'Just be nice to him all morning, and we'll sneak away when we can,' says Ted.

'OK.'

When we reach Happy, he pulls me in for the world's biggest hug.

'How's my favourite English woman?' he asks.

'I'm great. We're having a lovely time.'

'I'm so glad. I hope you like the trip this morning. It's an astonishing place; you'll see old St Lucia in its natural state. Jump in.'

'Are we the only ones?' I ask. I'm not surprised. There is a bar in the middle of the pool, for Christ's sake. Why would anyone leave to see a crumbly church?

'Yes, it's better that way. I can give you my full attention and show you everything.'

'Great,' I say. And off we go. We trundle through the beautiful St Lucian countryside, and I hang out of the window and take photographs that I know will be terrible but can't stop taking...just in case that *one* photo turns out to be amazing.

The lush greenery and vibrant flowers rush by in a blur.

'It's very remote, isn't it? I tell you what, if you wanted to kill someone and bury the body, this is where you'd come.'

I feel myself stiffen in my seat. A chill runs down my spine at Happy's casual mention of murder.

I glance at Ted, and he puts his arm around me. His touch is meant to be comforting, but it does little to ease the knot of tension in my stomach.

'Good job I'm a mean fighter, isn't it?' says Ted, aggressively.

'Yes, you can protect us all,' says Happy with a gurgling laugh. 'In all seriousness, though, it's quite safe here - no wild animals or anything to be scared of.'

We climb out of the car and Ted stands next to Happy, pulling himself to full height so he towers over him. I can see the muscles in Ted's jaw clench as he sizes up our guide, a silent battle of wills playing out between them.

'Right then. It's steep at the beginning, but it flattens out a bit. We'll walk 5km up the hill, stopping halfway so I can show you the church, then we'll head to the burial ground. We'll try and get back by down by midday so we're not walking when it's really hot.'

Midday? Four hours walking up a goddamn hill? I look at Ted, but he's too busy showing Happy how big he is to see my distress. I feel a flare of annoyance at his posturing, but I push it down, knowing that we need to present a united front.

We begin our ascent with Ted and Happy chatting while I amble behind. Ted asks Happy what he did yesterday evening, but Happy avoids the question. 'Look there,' says our guide, pointing ahead to a beautiful cluster of parakeets in the brightest green. As we move closer, they fly up into the air, like a puff of green smoke. The sight is breathtaking, a momentary reprieve from the heavy tension in the air.

'They're beautiful,' I say.

A few steps on, and we come across more. The more I look, the more I see. The parakeets are everywhere, filling the place with colour. On the branches of the trees, they look like leaves or moss. Their presence feels almost magical.

'Can I take one home?' I ask Happy, my mood having been considerably lifted by the sight of them.

'The most beautiful parrots you've ever seen are in the rainforest itself. Hopefully will catch sight of them. They have every colour on them... Vibrant blues, reds, yellows and greens. You will not believe your eyes.'

'This is lovely,' I say to Ted. 'I'm so glad I made you come.'

My husband treats me to a withering look.

'OK, we are at the first point,' says Happy.

I can't believe it. Have we been walking for a couple of kilometres? It's amazing how quickly time flies when you're watching the birds.

'This is a church. It is hundreds of years old. Let me tell you an interesting story about it...'

The tropical sun casts a warm glow over the lush green hillsides. The air is thick with the sweet fragrances of exotic blooms, and the earthy aroma of the dense rainforest surrounds us. I take a deep breath, letting the scents fill my lungs and trying to let the tranquillity of the setting soothe my frayed nerves.

'Look down there,' he says, pointing to a stony path

leading to the crumbling remains of an old stone church. There is ivy climbing its ancient walls.

'This church lies in ruins now, but centuries ago it was the heart of a small village. However, the graveyard where the villagers were laid to rest is at the top of this hill.'

He points up the hillside, where more weathered stone structures peek through the lush foliage. The sight is both beautiful and haunting, a reminder of the impermanence of life and the secrets that can be buried with the dead.

'Come on, I have much to show you,' he says.

As we continue the upward trek, I notice a strange pattern in the stones underfoot - pairs of them every few yards, as if marking the way. The stones are worn smooth by time and the elements, but their placement feels deliberate, like a code waiting to be deciphered.

'Those stones tell a wonderful story,' Happy explains. 'You see when a villager passed away, their body would be carried up this hillside path from the church to be buried in the graveyard at the summit. If those carrying the body grew weary and had to rest, placing the body down, they would carefully mark that spot with stones because it was believed that wherever the body briefly touched the earth after leaving the church's consecrated ground, that is where the soul detached itself to continue onward to the afterlife. So these pairs of stones serve as tiny grave markers for where souls took their departure along this solemn procession.'

His words paint a vivid picture in my mind, and I can almost see the ghostly figures of the villagers making their way up the hill, their grief etched into the very stones beneath our feet.. The stones seem very close.

'Do these mark the bodies of children?' I ask.

'Nope,' says Happy, coming to stand next to me. 'They are adults.'

The diminutive size of the makeshift grave outlines hints at the modest statures of the island's former inhabitants.

'That's incredible. I'm so glad we came,' I say again while Ted raises his eyebrows so high they threaten to get lost in his hairline.

'It's an incredible place,' says Happy, looking as proud as a parent showing off his child's glowing school report. 'You wouldn't imagine we were just outside Castries, would you?'

Once we reach the top, the sun breaks through to reveal an ancient graveyard. Stone crosses and weathered crypts blanket the sacred ground, each engraved with the names of those who now make this tranquil place their final resting spot.

'Take a look round if you like,' says Happy. 'We shouldn't stay too long because it's going to get very hot soon, but by all means - take a look.'

Ted and I wander around. I'm looking down and admiring the scenes while Ted closely monitors Happy, mumbling about the irony of the guy bringing us to a graveyard. I can't help but share Ted's unease, the coincidence of Happy bringing us to a place so closely associated with death feeling a little too on the nose given the events of the previous night.

'There's one good thing about all this, though. We're very near to Castries, where the train station is. I can get Happy to drop me off on the way back through.'

'Drop us off,' I reply. My voice is firm, leaving no room for argument. I'm not about to let Ted face whatever lies ahead alone, no matter how much he might want to protect me.

Once we've walked the length of the place, we head back to where Happy was standing, but there's no sign of him.

We wander around a little, hoping to spot him when, suddenly, he reappears.

'Ready to go?' he asks.

'Sure. Where did you go to? We've been looking for you.'

'Nowhere. Now then, let's head off.'

All three of us stride down the hill and back to the car. Once we're there, Ted introduces his request straight away.

'Thanks very much for taking us, Happy. We've had a great time. Can I just ask a favour of you?'

'Of course. Go ahead.'

'Would you mind dropping us in town on the way back? We haven't visited Castries and wouldn't mind a quick look around. We'll have lunch and jump in a cab back.'

'Sure,' he says, looking in the rear-view mirror. 'Is there anywhere in particular you'd like to go?'

'Just get a general look around the place. Nothing specific.'

'OK. Well, the place isn't as safe as Lobster Bay. This is a poor area, and there's quite a lot of crime. Do be careful. I can wait for you somewhere and drive you back if you'd prefer.'

'No, it's fine. Honestly, we'll be OK.'

Happy clearly doesn't think it will be OK, given the number of times he suggests staying and waiting for us, but Ted manages to convince him, and eventually, he drops us in the centre of Castries and says he looks forward to seeing us when we get back.'

Now it's time to see what on earth is in the locker. My

palms feel clammy around the mysterious key. The weight of it feels heavy in my hand, a tangible reminder of the unknown that lies ahead. My heart races as I imagine what secrets the locker might hold, and I can feel the adrenaline coursing through my veins.

The station is bustling with trains arriving and departing, conductors shouting out arrivals over the PA system. I scan the signs, zeroing in on the row of lockers near the south entrance - just where the 'X' lies on the map. The noise and chaos of the station fade into the background as I focus on our goal, my senses heightened by the knowledge that we are so close to discovering the truth.

'This way!' I grab Ted's hand, urgently pulling him along. We weave through the crowds until we stand in front of the lock boxes, which I count through.

'Eight...nine...ten. This is it!'

With trembling fingers, I insert the key into the lock and turn it. The latch clicks open with a heavy thunk, and I swing the small door wide. I feel my breath catch in my throat as I peer inside. A black sports duffel sits alone on the locker's bottom shelf. Ted snatches it out before I can react, heading for the exit at a brisk stride. I hurry along behind, throwing furtive glances in all directions. The bag feels like a live grenade in Ted's hands, a ticking time bomb that could explode at any moment and shatter the fragile illusion of normalcy we've been clinging to.

Ted stuffs the bag into the sports bag he has with him, and we rush out of the station and into the street to try and flag down a cab.

There are no cabs to be seen anywhere. The streets are eerily empty, as if the city itself is holding its breath, waiting for the inevitable fallout from our discovery.

'Perhaps it's dangerous to flag down cars here,' I say. 'We should have hired a car. We might be in real danger.'

The reality of our situation begins to sink in, and I feel a cold sweat break out on the back of my neck. We're in over our heads, and the weight of the unknown presses down on me like a physical burden.

As we start to panic about ever getting home, a pickup truck pulls up alongside us. The window is lowered to reveal Happy sitting there. His sudden appearance sends a jolt of fear through me, and I instinctively take a step back, my hand reaching for Ted's.

'Leaving already?'

'Yes, we decided that you were right. It's quite dangerous, and I think we both fancy an afternoon by the pool.'

'Sure, hop in,' he says. We clamber aboard and Happy pulls out back into the traffic. The air in the cab is thick with tension, and I can feel Happy's eyes on us in the rear-view mirror, watching, assessing.

It was handy that I took a phone call then, or I'd be halfway back to the hotel by now,' says Happy.

I look over at Ted and can see he's holding the bag so tightly in his grasp that I can see his knuckles go white and the veins in his forearms straining. I know he's thinking the same thing I am - that Happy knows more than he's letting on,

Once we get back to the hotel and into our room, we set the bag on the bed with shaky movements. The black duffel seems to absorb all the light in the room.

'Let's leave it for a minute,' says Ted.

I drop my voice to a whisper.

'No. We have to know what we're dealing with here.'

The urgency in my voice surprises even me, but I know

that we can't afford to waste any more time. Whatever secrets the bag holds, we need to face them head-on.

I unzip the bag slowly, and brightly coloured fabric tumbles out - seemingly just women's clothes. A blue sundress, jean shorts, a windsurfing t-shirt, and a green dress. But I know there has to be more. The clothes feel like a decoy, a distraction from the true purpose of the bag.

My heart pounds in my chest as I dig deeper, my fingers trembling with a mix of fear and anticipation. I excavate each garment one by one, running my fingers along the folds, probing for hidden surprises. A swimming costume, goggles... and that's when I feel it—something hard and cylindrical concealed within a cream sweater.

The object is cold and unyielding beneath my fingertips, and I feel a sense of dread wash over me as I realize what it must be. The metal object burns the pads of my fingers like an electric shock. I pull it out of the bag and watch Ted's eyes widen, his pupils swallowing the hazel irises. His reaction confirms my worst fears, and I feel a wave of nausea rise in my throat as I stare at the weapon in my hand.

With a steadying breath, I extract the object fully. A pistol, the steel barrel glinting like a scorpion's stinger under the kitchen lights.

The gun feels heavy and alien in my grip, a tangible reminder of the danger we've stumbled into. I've never held a weapon before, and the power it represents terrifies me.

'Holy shit...' Ted's curse hangs in the air as I quickly stash the gun aside and dig deeper into the tangle of concealing clothes. My movements are frantic now, my heart racing as I search for any other hidden surprises.

Another hard lump beneath the folds of a floral skirt. I tug it out to reveal a knife.

'Christ.'

The two weapons lie before us in mocking display amidst the pastel fabrics. Ted drags a hand down his face, the tendons straining in his neck. I can see the fear and disbelief etched into every line of his face, a mirror of my own emotions. We're in over our heads, and we both know it.

My heart is thundering against my ribcage. Whatever underworld is operating from the shadows...we are now inextricably entangled. I swallow hard against the lump of dread in my throat as our new reality solidifies around us.

The weight of the unknown presses down on me, suffocating in its intensity. No turning back now. Forces are in motion that can swallow us whole if we don't tread carefully.

I meet Ted's wild-eyed stare, seeing the same questions racing behind his eyes. We're in this together, for better or worse.

Whose weapons are these? What game are we caught up in? Can we emerge from this unscathed?

The questions swirl in my mind, a maelstrom of fear and uncertainty that threatens to pull me under.

CHAPTER
FOURTEEN

Fans whir on the ceiling, designed to keep the room cool and well-aired, but it isn't enough. The sickly heat is oppressive and draining. I can't breathe properly. Fear and confusion have left me nauseous; the acidic taste of bile rising in the back of my throat threatens to spill over at any moment.

I swing open the windows, clutching the window frame as I look out onto the gardens, bursting with colour and life. The vibrant hues of the tropical flowers and the lush greenery seem to mock the darkness that has invaded our lives. I take a big gulp of air, breathing out slowly, trying to steady my racing heart and calm the storm of emotions raging inside me.

'For God's sake, Mary. Be careful,' says Ted, rushing across the room and dragging me back. He slams the window shut and draws the blinds, turning to look at me, holding me tightly by the shoulders. Fear is etched across his face, and his eyes are wide with a mix of concern and frustration.

'The whole of the criminal underworld might be watching us. You can't just open the window.'

'I know Ted, but I feel sick. And we've done nothing wrong.'

'I know we haven't, but convincing anyone of that will be very difficult.'

'Why will it? Let's just tell them the truth. We're innocent - that's the end of it.'

'And how compelling will our cries of innocence sound when they come in and see thousands of dollars in the safe?'

'But we're innocent,' I repeat as I sit on the huge, soft bed. Rays of sunlight escape through the blinds and cast lines across the white Egyptian cotton sheets in front of me, like the bars of a cell.

We're in a beautiful room in the most wonderful hotel we've ever seen on a stunning Caribbean Island full of beauty and joy. This is supposed to be the holiday of a lifetime. It's our honeymoon, for goodness' sake.

'How on earth has it all gone so wrong?' I ask Ted, my voice barely above a whisper, the weight of our predicament pressing down on me like a physical burden.

'We got unlucky,' he says, coming over to hold my hands. His touch is a small comfort in the midst of the chaos swirling around us.

'Do you think this Cara Jeffries is some kind of assassin?'

'It sounds to me like she's gone missing after getting entangled with some very dodgy people.'

'Why are there no articles online about her disappearance? Why is no one at the hotel talking about it? The whole thing is insane.'

'Perhaps the hotel has kept it quiet because they don't want to put off potential guests?'

'But that's terrible. Surely, they should be putting posters of her everywhere and trying to find her. What about her family and friends?' I say.

'Perhaps they don't even know that she's gone missing?'

'Oh my God, do you think they might not know?'

'If no one has told them, they couldn't possibly know,' says Ted.

'The poor girl. I wonder where she is. She must be terrified.'

'If she's still alive.'

'We have to try and find her,' I say, a newfound determination surging through me, momentarily overpowering the fear and uncertainty that have been my constant companions.

'How?'

'I don't know. Perhaps we should take everything we have to the police? Or perhaps we should confront Happy? Or that policeman who is staying here...Barney. He might be worth talking to. What do you think?'

I look at Ted, searching his face for any sign of agreement or support, desperate for a way out of the nightmare we've found ourselves in.

There's a heavy silence, the weight of our choices hanging in the air between us, each option fraught with its own set of risks and uncertainties.

'I think we should try and find this woman,' I say again, my voice steady and resolute, a flicker of hope igniting in my chest. 'If you won't help me, I'll do it alone.'

CHAPTER
FIFTEEN

Cara's story: 28th June
10 days earlier

'Stop,' said Katherine, her voice cutting through the haze of Cara's sobs. 'You've got to get a grip of yourself, Cara. I can hardly hear you above all the sobbing. What on earth has happened?'

'Every penny I inherited from my aunty has gone. Every bit of it. There's nothing left, and it's all my stupid fault.'

Cara's voice trembled, each word punctuated by a hiccupping breath as she fought to regain control.

'How have you lost it? You're not making any sense at all.'

'Because I made the stupidest mistake ever.'

'OK, try and stop crying for a minute, and tell me what's happened.'

Cara took a deep breath.

'I invested all my money in the scheme I told you about. The one that Tajo recommended.'

'But you said that scheme was good.'

'I thought it was.'

'Money can go up and down, Cara. Perhaps it's just a blip?'

'No, it's not. I looked on my phone just now, and it says all the money has been taken out, and the account has closed down.'

'Perhaps the market was trending downward, so the investor pulled it out. I don't know, but it can't have disappeared. I'm sure it's there somewhere. They can't close it and remove all the money without your authorisation.'

'I know, but someone has.'

'What has Tajo said?'

'I can't get hold of him. He's nowhere to be found. I've been calling him all morning. It's like he's disappeared off the face of the Earth; there's nothing, no one exists. I don't understand it.'

Desperation tinged her words, the unanswered calls and messages echoing in her mind like a cruel taunt.

'What do you mean 'no one exists'?'

Katherine could hear Rachel moving around in the hallway and called her into the room.

'I can't get hold of anyone at all. No one.'

'When did you last see Tajo?'

'Last night. We were heading back when he realised he'd left his wallet on the boat and had to rush back to get it. He was going to come back to mine but then sent a text telling me he was going to head home and he'd come and take me to breakfast in the morning, but he hasn't turned up, and I can't reach him, and I've just seen that all my money has disappeared. What am I going to do?'

The words tumbled out in a rush, Cara's voice rising with each passing second, the helplessness of her situation threatening to overwhelm her.

Katherine looked at Rachel, a silent conversation passing between them as they tried to find the right words to comfort their distraught friend.

'Cara, it's Rache here. Look - is there anything we can do?'

'I don't know,' said Cara, her voice thick with tears and snot, the words bubbling and slobbering as she struggled to speak. 'I don't know what's going on.'

'Do you have anyone out there who could help you?'

'No,' said Cara, the word hanging in the air, small and pitiful.

'Have you spoken to the police?'

'No, I rang you first. I'm scared to go to the police.'

'Why?'

'I don't know. They're not like the police at home. People keep saying they can't be trusted and are as bad as the criminals.'

'Who said that?'

'Everyone. Happy, the guy I work for, showed me an article in which it says that the police have been going around killing criminals. They have 'death lists'; it all sounds awful.' A shiver ran down Cara's spine at the memory, the words on the page searing into her mind, a stark reminder of the dangerous world she found herself in.

'Have you spoken to Happy?'

'No, not this morning.'

'OK, let's make a plan,' said Katherine, her voice steady and calm, a lifeline in the chaos of Cara's thoughts.

'First you need to find Tajo. Have you ever been to his house?'

'Yes, but only once. It was up in the hills somewhere. I don't know whether I'd find it again.'

'OK, what about his job?'

'He works for himself doing investments and financial stuff.'

'OK, well, finding his house will be crucial. Can you see whether you can work out where his house is?'

'OK, I'll try. We went for lunch at this restaurant, then walked over to it.'

'Right, so if you can find the restaurant, you should be able to find him. Do you remember what the restaurant was called?'

'No idea.'

'Why don't you get a list together of all the restaurants in the area and look through them, see whether any memories can be triggered?' said Rachel.

'Yes - good idea. Then head for the boat to see whether anyone there can help,' said Katherine.

'And the financial adviser. Try him,' said Rachel.

'Oh yes—that's a good call. Try him. Did he give you his card?' Katherine asked.

'Yes,' said Cara, a flicker of relief in her voice at the thought of a tangible lead.

'And what about all those friends of his you met last night? Did any of them say where they worked or lived? Any cards or anything?'

'No. I mean - it was a drinks party. People weren't handing out business cards. Oh, hang on. One of the guys did. I've just remembered. Chuckles gave me a card. I'll find it.'

'Do any of the people at the water sports place know him?'

'No, he never met any of my friends there. Oh, hang on. Yes, he did. He met Tom. They didn't like each other.'

'OK, love. Well, I think you need to talk to him. Perhaps this Tom will come with you to find Tajo?'

Cara thought about lovely, kind Tom, his warm smile and gentle eyes a stark contrast to the cold, calculating gazes of the men on the boat. She didn't really want Tom mixed up in all this. She'd ask him whether he'd seen Tajo anywhere but wouldn't involve him.

'Yes, he might. And I've just had another thought...I met these two guys on the flight over; they were lovely. I might call them and see whether they can help.'

'OK, be careful, won't you, love. I can't stand the thought of you all out there on your own trying to track this guy down.'

Katherine's voice was thick with worry, the miles between them suddenly feeling like an impossible gulf.

'I will, I promise.'

Cara pushed open the heavy doors to the boat house, the hinges creaking in protest as the acrid aroma of petrol and fresh paint assaulted her nostrils, the fumes stinging her eyes and catching in her throat.

'Shouldn't you leave these doors open?' she asked. 'You're going to collapse with all these toxic fumes.'

Cara could see Tom leaning up against the wall on the far side, his tall frame silhouetted against the sunlight streaming in through the windows, while the mechanics and boat crew worked.

'I thought you were off today,' he said, his voice warm and familiar, a balm to her frayed nerves.

'I am, but I'm having a bit of a nightmare. Can I talk to you?'

'Of course. Everything OK?' he asked as he led her into

the small room at the back of the boat shed. Pots of paints, varnish and sealant sat all around, their pungent scents mingling with the smell of salt and sea that clung to the spare sails on the floor and ropes stacked in the corner.

Cara had always been taught that tidy sailing was safe sailing and that equipment should always be looked after properly, particularly ropes and sails, but here in St Lucia, everything was relaxed; no one took things quite as seriously as they had in Devon, where she's learned to surf and sail on brisk mornings before heading out to work.

'Come on then, sweetheart, what's bothering you?'

Cara breathed deeply, the air shuddering in her lungs as she fought back the tears that threatened to spill over, hoping not to cry as she relayed the tale.

'Shit. Why did you invest all that money?'

'I don't know. I got carried away. I'm an idiot, that's why.'

'And it was Tajo that persuaded you?'

'Well, yes. It was his friends. On that boat last night with all these wankers, and they were all so rich, and I decided that I wanted to be rich too.' Shame washed over her in waves, the memory of her own greed and naivety making her cheeks burn.

'OK. Right. There's someone I need to call. We'll do everything we can to sort this out.' Tom picked up the phone and rang Happy. Cara listened as Tom explained what had happened. She felt even more of an idiot when she heard the whole thing clearly explained, the reality of her actions laid bare in the harsh light of day.

'He's on his way,' said Tom, giving Cara a huge hug. 'Let's see what we can do, eh?'

'You knew he was trouble, didn't you?'

'He seemed a bit edgy. A bit too rough and unsophisticated for someone like you.'

Tom's words were gentle, but the truth behind them stung.

She smiled at him.

'Thank you,' she said.

She needed to be told that she was sophisticated right now because that was exactly what she didn't feel, her confidence shattered by the events of the past few hours.

The sound of running alerted them to the arrival of Happy, who appeared in front of them, his chest heaving as he fought to catch his breath, sweat glistening on his brow.

'I came as quickly as I could. What's happened? Cara - tell me everything.'

Cara ran through the story in as much detail as she could remember, the words spilling out of her in a torrent, the relief of unburdening herself to someone she trusted almost overwhelming.

'What's his name?'

'His name's Tajo.'

'I've never heard of him,' said Happy, shaking his head.

'Tajo? No, it doesn't ring a bell. Have you got a picture?'

'Yes,' she said, remembering the photos she'd taken on the boat. She rummaged in her bag for her phone. Then she remembered...she'd had to remove the photos.

The memory of them making her take the pictures off her phone made her feel distinctly uneasy, a cold sense of dread settling in the pit of her stomach. What had felt like overzealousness at the time now felt like preparation for a crime.

'You do know him. I've just remembered - he mentioned you and said the two of you didn't get on.'

'What was the guy's name again?'

'Tajo. I used to call him Taj.'

'And he told you he and I didn't get on?'

'Yes. We always met by the cove, and if he stayed over, we'd return after dark. He didn't want his problems with you to cause me problems at work.'

'I honestly don't know what this is all about. I don't think I've fallen out with anyone, and I'm sure I'd remember if I had.'

Happy's brow furrowed in confusion, his eyes searching Cara's face for answers she didn't have. Cara sighed. There was so much about this that made no sense at all.

'I don't like the sound of this at all,' said Happy. 'Have you been to the police?'

'No, I hear all sorts of bad things about the police in St Lucia. In fact, you've told me lots of bad things about the police in St Lucia.'

'Well, yes - it's not always straightforward. But you might have to go to them if you have been robbed. What was the name of the boat?'

'Omeros.'

'I don't know it. I'll find out whatever I can. Do you want to come with us, and we'll do some investigating?'

'Yes, please. I don't want to stay here on my own. Also - I have these...' Cara handed him the two business cards. The first was the one given to her by Jesus, the personal finance expert and the second was given to her by Rok Chuckles. Happy looked at them and put them into his pocket, his expression darkening as he studied the names.

'Do you remember anything distinctive about the guys?'

'Yes, the financial adviser was tiny and in a suit that was far too big for him. He looked like a child dressing up in his dad's clothes. Rok Chuckles was horrible. He was mean and nasty with a big tattoo of a lion on his face and this enormous yellow ring.'

'Yellow?' Happy looked worried, his eyes widening in recognition, a flicker of fear crossing his features.

'Yes, he also had a yellow bandana in his top pocket.'

'Shit. I know exactly who these guys are.'

'Do you?'

'Yes. They're a nasty gang. I've come across them before. They are called Lyon. Basically 'lions' in Creole. They are a nasty, murdering bunch of thugs, but I do know someone who might be able to help. In the meantime, let's go and see what we can find out about the addresses on the cards.'

The three of them climbed into the back of Happy's pickup truck and drove to Marigot. There was no sign of the boat. Happy got out of the pickup truck and went to talk to the men manning the tenders at the harbour, his voice low and urgent as he questioned them, his body tense with barely contained anger.

They told him that Omeros was not based there. It had been hired for an afternoon but there's no record of who chartered it.

'It'll be impossible to find out. The men rent boats, change their names, and then disappear. They might never come back.'

'Right, come on,' said Happy, raising the business cards in the air. 'Let's find these guys. Jesus first.'

Happy headed into Castries, the rough part of the city, to search for the addresses on the business cards.

'I hope we find them straight away,' said Cara, but she saw Happy glance at Tom and knew he was highly doubtful that they would ever find them. Her eyes filled with tears.

What if they never found them? What if all her money was lost? She felt a sharp stab of pain and anger at herself.

Had she wasted all her inheritance, the last tangible link to her beloved aunt, on a foolish dream of easy money and a better life?

Christ, this barely seemed possible. It was like a nightmare being reenacted in daylight.

They found the area that supposedly housed the financial services company. It was a very rough place, in the docks, and nowhere likely to have a financial institution. They saw the building that was supposed to house the company, but it was half-fallen down.

'There's no point getting out and looking,' said Happy. 'This is such a rough area. It's not here.'

'Can we check the address on Chuckles' card?' she asked. 'You know – just incase.'

'Of course,' said Happy, but the address took them to a dilapidated house a short while away. They got out this time and walked around the ruins of a burnt-out house. The charred remains of the structure loomed before them, a stark reminder of the destruction and violence that lurked beneath the surface of this seemingly idyllic island paradise.

Cara's heart sank as she surveyed the scene, the last embers of hope flickering and dying in her chest.

'I'm sorry,' said Happy. 'I need to make some calls and check a few people out. You go home and stay on the hotel grounds, and we'll talk tomorrow, OK?'

'But, what about Tajo's house in the hills. Shall we try that?'

'Do you have an address?'

'No.'

'Do you have any idea where it is?'

'It was kind of near a café. I don't know. I can't remember. There were these hibiscus bushes. It smelled amazing.'

'I'll drop you home, and you can think about where it might be. It sounds to me like he just picked a smart house and pretended that he owned it, but try to remember, and we'll go and pay it a visit tomorrow.'

'Sure,' she said.

That night Cara paced around her room, her mind racing as she tried to make sense of the events of the past few days. The once comforting walls of her room now felt like a prison, the tropical beauty outside her window a cruel mockery of the turmoil that raged within her.

What would she do if she couldn't find the money? How would she pay for her master's course? She wouldn't be able to do it. What would she do?

The questions churned in her mind, an endless loop of despair and self-recrimination. She thought of her aunt, of the sacrifices she had made to leave Cara this money, of the trust she had placed in her to use it wisely. The weight of her failure pressed down on her, suffocating her, stealing the very air from her lungs. She cried herself to sleep, her pillow damp with the tears of broken dreams and shattered hopes, the sound of her own sobs echoing in the emptiness of her room as she finally succumbed to exhaustion.

CHAPTER
SIXTEEN

2 9th June

As soon as Cara woke, the crushing reality of what had happened hit her full-on. The weight of her losses pressed down on her chest, making it hard to breathe. The realisation that she had been duped, that her trust had been so utterly betrayed, left a bitter taste in her mouth.

She'd lost everything. She'd lost Tajo, with whom she thought she'd have a future, and she'd lost every penny of her money: the money that was supposed to see her through the summer in elegant style, then pay for her master's degree and allow her to make a small foothold on the property ladder when she graduated.

Her dreams, once so vivid and within reach, now lay shattered at her feet, the fragments of her hopes and aspirations cutting her to the core. All gone. She started to cry as images of Aunty Susan came into her mind. The guilt gnawed at her insides. How could she have been so blind, so naive?

The more she thought about it, the more she realised that all the signs were there right from the start. Why would someone like Tajo want someone like her? She was just a silly girl, playing at being a sophisticated woman. She had fallen for his charm, smooth words, and empty promises, and now she was paying the price. She'd been so incredibly naive.

She punched the pillow in anger and sat up aggressively. The sudden movement sent a jolt of pain through her head, a physical manifestation of the turmoil that raged within her. She had to get the money back, somehow. This was so ridiculous. People couldn't just come and take all your money.

There had to be a way, a solution, a path forward. She couldn't let them win, couldn't let them destroy her life so completely. She would go to the police station first thing and tell them about everything that happened. Then she would call everyone she knew in the UK and ask them whether they knew anyone who could help. She scanned her brain for thoughts of people at home, people who worked in banking... Anyone who understood this sort of thing. But she could think of no one.

Her social circles were dominated by students and those who enjoyed literature, not sophisticated banker types who could spot fraud in a second and understood how to unravel financial corruption. The realisation of her own ignorance, her own lack of knowledge and resources, settled like a lead weight in her stomach.

She lay back on her bed, flicking through her phone's address book, just in case there was someone in there who could offer even the slightest glimmer of hope. Then she tracked through her WhatsApp messages. There was just a pile of messages between her and the girls.

The sight of their happy, carefree conversations felt like a cruel mockery now, a reminder of a life that seemed so far away, so utterly out of reach.

That's when she saw them... pictures of the guys on the boat. The women had made her remove the pictures from her phone, but she had already sent them to the girls. There they were, sitting in a WhatsApp message—Tajo was as clear as day, and you could see other faces around the bar. They offered a tantalising glimpse of a world she had been so briefly a part of, a world that had ultimately betrayed her. Surely this would help to find them.

A flicker of hope ignited in her chest, a small spark amidst the darkness that threatened to engulf her. Maybe, just maybe, these pictures held the key to unravelling the mystery to get her life back on track.

She rang Tom straight away.

'I've got pictures of the guys who stole my money. There are pictures on the boat, and you can see Tajo's face clearly,' she said. 'Can I bring them to show you?'

'Don't worry. I'll come to you,' he said. 'Stay there, I'm on my way. I'll bring Happy.'

Tom and Happy sat on the edge of the bed and looked at the pictures on her phone.

'The other thing I remembered is – Tajo is a major investor in the hotel. He's on the board. We should easily be able to find him.'

Happy's expression was grave; his eyes narrowed in concentration as he studied the images.

'Well, this Tajo guy is right that he and I fell out, but his name isn't Tajo. He's made that up. It's Linus.'

He looked at Cara.

'Linus is very dangerous, 'as are all the guys in this photo. Does anyone know you have these photos on here?'

'No.'

'Can you send them to me via WhatsApp, then take them off your phone?'

He was adopting the same aggressive tone as the women on the boat. 'Do that now.'

'Why are you saying this?' she asked. 'I don't understand why you want me to remove them. They are useful. They're the only evidence I have about who is behind all this.''

'I know who is behind all this,' said Happy. 'I'm asking you to remove the pictures from your phone completely.'

Why was Happy being so odd with her? What sense did it make for her to take her pictures off the phone when she would need them if she went to the police? They were the only evidence she had that Tajo had ever existed. A sense of unease crept up her spine, a nagging feeling that something wasn't right, that there were forces at play that she didn't fully understand.

'Please take them off your phone,' said Happy. Cara sat there, looking bewildered until Happy took her phone, forwarded the pics to himself, deleted the photos and gave it back to her. 'I'm sorry. I know you don't understand, but you must trust me.'

'We need to go,' said Tom. 'They'll be waiting.'

'Who will be waiting?' asked Cara. She was aware that lots of things were going on behind her back, and while she trusted Tom implicitly, she wanted to know what was happening. The secrecy, the cryptic comments, and the sense that everyone knew more than they were letting on. This was driving her mad, fuelling the paranoia and fear that already gripped her heart.

'Have you got any friends you can spend the day with today?' asked Happy.

'Um. Well, not really. I'm supposed to be working.'

'I've signed you off. Don't worry about that.'

'OK. Well, I met two guys on the plane on the way over and said I'd catch up with them. I could call them?'

'Good idea,' said Happy. 'See whether you can meet up with them, and we'll keep in touch by phone.'

'What are you two going to be doing?'

'We're going to try and sort this out for you. Send us a text to let us know where you will be.'

∼

It was 10 am when she got together with Robbie and Scott at Sunshaker Cafe. She'd told Tom where she was going and now longed to get the view of the two men she'd met on the plane.

The sun was already beating down mercilessly, and the heat was oppressive and stifling, but Cara hardly noticed. Her mind was consumed with the events of the past few days, the questions swirling in her head, and the fear gnawing at her insides.

'This sounds like a complete scam,' said Robbie.

'I'm starting to feel the same thing; I wish I'd never come out to this stupid place,' said Cara. The words tasted bitter on her tongue, reflecting the regret and self-recrimination that consumed her.

'Come on,' said Scott. 'Let's go to the police. This is getting too complicated for us to deal with. It makes me very uncomfortable. You've lost a ton of money, and the boyfriend you were seeing suddenly doesn't exist. You have to report it.'

'But the police are dodgy.'

'I don't believe every police officer in St Lucia is corrupt. And look at the people who are telling you that the police are corrupt – Tajo doesn't exist anymore, and Happy just deleted from your phone the only evidence you had. Are you 100% sure that Happy isn't part of all this? Because I think he is,' said Robbie.

'No, I don't think so. Not for a minute. He was really helpful yesterday.'

'I'm just not convinced, and - anyway - regardless of that, we need to do what we think is the best thing, and as far as I'm concerned, that's going to the police.'

'Shall I let Happy know?'

'No,' said Scott.

'Yes,' said Robbie.

Cara looked at them both. The conflicting advice only heightened her confusion and uncertainty. She felt like a puppet, her strings being pulled by unseen hands, her fate no longer her own to control.

'If you tell him that you're going to the police, he might turn aggressive,' said Scott.

'No,' said Robbie. 'If you tell him you're going to the police, he'll be forced to tell you what's happening. Remember, he doesn't want you to go to the police. He's been strongly advising you against it. As long as you do what he asks, he has you in the palm of his hand. You need to understand why he's behaving like this.'

'So you genuinely think that Happy is involved? I consider myself a good character judge, and I never had him pegged as a troublemaker. He's helping me.'

Robbie and Scott looked at her. 'A good judge of character?'

'Okay, yes – Tajo was a bad judgement call.'

'The very worst judgement call.'

'Call Happy and tell him you're going to the police,' said Robbie. 'We'll stay with you and come to the station with you.'

'Let's have breakfast first, then I'll decide,' said Cara. She was pretty sure she wouldn't be able to eat anything. Her stomach was churning, and the thought of putting any food in it made her feel quite nauseous. The anxiety, the fear, the uncertainty - it was all taking its toll, physically and emotionally. She felt like a shell of her former self.

She ordered a fruit salad and pushed it around the plate. Just as she pushed it away unable even to pretend to eat it, a text arrived from Tom asking her to meet him on the corner of the road near the pretty cafe they were currently in.

Now she just had to leave Robbie and Scott without arousing suspicion.

'Listen. I'll be back in half an hour, but there's something I have to do,' she said.

'What? What do you have to do?' asked Scott.

'You'll have to trust me, but I promise I'll be back, and I won't be long.'

Cara began the short walk along the cliffs and saw Tom sitting in Happy's truck.

'Get in,' he said.

Cara jumped into the passenger seat and looked at her friend.

'We can get your money back, but we need to get you out of the area for a few days because once they realise what's happened, your life will be in danger. We'll pack clothes to take with you and leave food every day. Once we feel it's safe, or we hear of any event that's taking place that will tie them all up, out of the way, we'll let you know, and we'll get you out of the country.'

'Oh my God.'

'Don't worry. It all sounds more dramatic than it is.'

'Yeah, well. It all sounds pretty dramatic.'

'Try to stay calm, and everything will be OK.'

'Can I call anyone?'

'No - they will be tracking your phone. We'll leave notes telling you what to do next. Just two key points to mention...when we decide it's safe for you to leave, we'll leave a note with the food we leave, telling you where a chunk of the money is. You'll collect that, which you need to use to buy your ticket home. Buy first class.'

'OK.'

'There will also be a small key and a map. The key will open a locker at St Lucia train station, and in there will be your phone, additional clothes and weapons.'

'Weapons?'

'Yes, don't go there unless you are worried, but it will be there if you need it.'

'Christ.'

'These are just Happy's security measures. He says that you having a gun in your possession will stop anyone attacking you.'

'But, I've never fired a gun. I wouldn't know what to do.'

'I know. And you won't have to fire it. If you want, you can just take your phone out of the locker and proceed without the bag, but there will also be a change of clothes there incase you think you need to change before going to the airport. The weapons are just extra security.'

Cara was crying and terrified as she was led up the mountain in the searing heat towards a small hut. Tom was behind, pushing her on.

'They will find me, I should've let them keep the money,' she thought, her mind racing with the possibilities of what lay ahead, each more terrifying than the last.

Tom urged her to move forward up the stark terrain across the rocky landscape, getting hotter as the sun rose. The stony ground cracking in the heat, he carried her bag and urged her to walk faster. 'Come on - Happy won't be very happy if you don't get a move on.' His words sent a chill down her spine, the implication clear - Happy was behind this, behind her suffering, behind the hell she now found herself in.

'Happy?'

The world seemed to tilt on its axis, the ground shifting beneath her feet as the true nature of her situation began to sink in. Was she being led to her death? Did he want her gone because she could identify the assailants? She stumbled forward, her body numb with fear and exhaustion.

'Just hurry up, for God's sake,' he said, as they walked past the ruins of an ancient church and further up to what looked like an old cemetery. A place of eternal rest, a final destination for so many, now serving as the backdrop for her hell. The symbolism was almost too much to bear, a cruel mockery of the life she had once known, the dreams she had once held so dear.

CHAPTER
SEVENTEEN

'What will we say to the police when we get there? We don't know anything about her,' said Scott as the two men clung on for dear life in the back of the taxi, which hurtled with reckless speed through the busy streets of Castries.

The city's vibrant colours and lively sounds blurred past the windows, starkly contrasting the gnawing fear gripping their hearts.

'We know she's missing,' said Robbie, his voice tight with worry. 'She disappeared from the café at about 11 this morning, and there's not been a word from her since.'

His mind raced with the possibilities, each more terrifying than the last, as he tried to make sense of Cara's sudden vanishing act.

'I guess,' said Scott, his brow furrowed in frustration. 'I wish we knew her friends and family or any more information to give the police.'

As they had waited that morning, and it had become increasingly unlikely that Cara would come back, the two of them had looked online for any sign of Cara Jeffries, but they weren't even sure how she spelled her surname, and they found no one on social media or listed on Google who looked at all like her.

The digital dead end only heightened their sense of unease, a nagging feeling that something was wrong. They had to report it.

'Here,' said the taxi driver. 'Good luck with the police.'

St Lucia's Central Police Station was a beautiful building. Its whitewashed walls and imposing entrance gave it colonial splendour, and its Royal Saint Lucia Police Force emblem sat proudly above the door, a symbol of authority and order amidst the chaos of the streets.

'So far, so good,' said Robbie, his eyes scanning the façade.

'What were you expecting?' Scott asked, raising an eyebrow.

'I don't know…something much scruffier and more threatening.'

'You're such a wimp,' Scott teased, trying to lighten the mood, but the humour fell flat in the face of their shared anxiety. Scott pulled open the door, allowing Robbie to enter the bustling reception area first. People were everywhere, all talking incredibly loudly and jostling for attention at the desk. Officers in the force's traditional navy-blue uniforms tried to calm people down, their voices rising above the din in an attempt to restore order.

Scott stood in line behind the crowd gathered around the front desk while Robbie studied the informational posters covering the walls, his eyes darting from one to the next, searching for any hint of what they should do in their situation.

'Hey, you. You in the jacket. Englishman. Come round here.'

The voice cut through the noise, sharp and authoritative, demanding attention. Scott walked around the rowdy group, his heart pounding as he approached the officer who had singled him out.

'How did you know I was English?' he asked, trying to keep his voice steady.

'You were queueing,' said the officer with a self-congratulatory smile, a hint of amusement flickering in his eyes.

'I'm Officer Victor Emanuel. What can I help you with?'

'Our friend has gone missing. She's disappeared, and we don't know what to do about it. We're not sure what the protocol is here. She's from England as well. Is there someone we can talk to?'

Scott's words tumbled out in a rush, the urgency of their situation bleeding into his voice.

'How long has she been missing?' asked the officer, picking up a pencil and looking sternly at Scott, his gaze piercing and unwavering.

'She's been gone since 11ish this morning,' Scott replied, his stomach churning with hope and dread.

The officer dropped the pencil, his expression shifting from one of concern to one of dismissal. 'Then she's not a missing person.'

Robbie joined Scott and stood silently by his side, a united front in the face of the officer's apparent indifference.

'But we're worried that something's happened to her. She was nervous and got this sudden call out of the blue. We'd like someone to investigate,' Scott pressed, his frustration mounting.

The officer shook his head, his jaw set in a stubborn line.

'Please. At least make a note of her name,' Robbie implored, his voice edged with desperation.

'OK, what's her name?' asked the officer, without reaching for his pencil.

'Cara. Cara Jeffries.'

The policeman stood completely still and stared at them, his eyes widening in recognition. 'Cara Jeffries?'

'Yes,' said Robbie and Scott in unison, their hearts leaping into their throats. 'Why do you look like that? Do you know her?' The questions hung in the air, heavy with implication.

CHAPTER
EIGHTEEN

'Come with me,' said the officer, lifting the wooden panel in the desk to allow them through. They followed the officer beyond the reception area, past an array of offices and into a small, windowless room that smelled of body odour and fear. The oppressive atmosphere closing in around them like a physical weight.

'Okay then, what have you got for me?' said the officer, his tone brusque and business-like. 'My name is Robbie, and this is Scott; we came over from England a few weeks ago and met a girl called Cara on the plane,' Robbie began, his voice shaking slightly as he recounted their story.

'How are you spelling that?' asked the police officer, his pen poised over a notepad.

'I assume it's C – A – R – A.' '

You assume?'

'We only met her on the plane. I never asked her to write her name down,' Robbie explained, feeling a flush of embarrassment creep up his neck.

'And what's her surname?' asked the officer, his pen still hovering over the paper.

'Jeffries. Her name is Cara Jeffries.'

'And she's gone missing, you say?'

The officer's tone was neutral, betraying no hint of the concern or urgency the situation warranted.

'Well, yes – we were with her having lunch. She'd had some bad news and was very nervous and jittery, then she got a message and ran off. She said she'd be back soon, but we haven't seen her since.

'We've been to the hotel where she lives, and there's no sign. Her clothes appear to have gone. But she never mentioned leaving when we saw her. I just don't know where she could be.'

Robbie's words spilled out.

'Hold on,' said the officer. He bolted out of the room, slammed the door behind him, and was gone for 10 minutes, leaving Robbie and Scott alone with their thoughts and the suffocating silence of the room.

'This is a good thing,' said Robbie, trying to convince himself as much as Scott. 'They're taking it seriously.'

'Yeah, It feels odd though. He's thrown by her name. Almost as if he knew her.'

'Perhaps other people have reported her missing...' Robbie suggested, grasping at straws.

'I wouldn't have thought so. We were the only people to see her when she left.'

Scott's mind raced with the implications, the pieces of the puzzle failing to fit together in any coherent way.

'We don't know that. She left us, and we don't know who she spoke to after that,' Robbie countered, trying to cling to any shred of hope, any possibility that Cara was safe and sound. The door opened, and the officer came in with another guy. The new guy was very broad and appeared menacing. If you were being attacked in the street, he's the police officer you'd want to come to your rescue. But if you were at the police reporting a missing person, he wasn't the person you would want to be in the room to confront you. His presence filled the small space, his bulk and demeanour projecting an aura of intimidation and control.

'I'm Officer Augustin Francis. Are you saying that Cara Jeffries has gone missing?' His voice was deep and commanding, his eyes boring into Robbie and Scott with an intensity that made them squirm. He leaned onto the desk so his shoulders flared out, making him look like a bull ready to charge.

'Yes, do you know Cara Jeffries?' Scott asked, his heart pounding in his chest as he searched the officer's face for any hint of recognition or concern.

'I know nothing about her,' said the officer, his expression unreadable. 'Why would I?'

Robbie and Scott exchanged glances, a silent communication passing between them, a shared sense of unease and confusion. This was odd. Not at all the expected response when they walked into the station.

'So, what happens now?' asked Robbie, his voice barely above a whisper.

'We usually have to wait 48 hours for someone to be missing before it's considered a missing person's investigation, but in these circumstances, we'll start making enquiries immediately. We'll need to take down details of everything you know.'

The officer's words offered a glimmer of hope, a reassurance that they were taking the situation seriously, but something about his tone and demeanour still felt off.

'To be honest, we've told you everything we know,' Scott admitted, feeling the weight of their own helplessness pressing down on him.

'I'm sure there are more details. Officer Francis here will take notes and assess the situation.' The dismissal in the officer's voice was clear.

'But we need to get out looking for her straight away. I think she may be in danger,' Robbie protested, his fear and frustration boiling over. The two officers glanced at one another.

'We will take action as soon as we have filed a missing person's report. I'll leave you with Officer Francis,' the first officer said, his tone brooking no argument as he turned and left the room, leaving Robbie and Scott alone with the imposing figure of Officer Francis.

The interview took longer than it should have, considering Robbie and Scott knew nothing about Cara Jeffries other than that her money had been stolen, and then she disappeared.

The officer asked questions about Cara's current whereabouts. It was interminable.

For the love of God, if I knew where she was, she wouldn't be a missing person, thought Robbie, but he bit back the sarcastic retort that danced on the tip of his tongue, knowing that antagonising the officer would do nothing to help Cara.

The frustration and helplessness he felt was mirrored in Scott's eyes, a shared sense of impotence. They kept repeating that they knew nothing about her home life or whether she was still on the island.

They didn't see how she could have left in that time, but that's all they had to offer. The words felt hollow and insufficient, a meagre offering in the face of Cara's disappearance and the growing sense of dread that filled the room.

'Did she know who had taken her money?' Officer Francis asked, his tone sharp and probing.

'No,' they replied, their voices flat and defeated.

'Are you sure?' The officer's eyes narrowed, his gaze piercing and accusatory.

'Yes, we're sure,' Scott said, his jaw clenching with barely controlled anger.

'OK, we'll be in touch,' said Officer Francis, his tone dismissive. 'Don't leave the country or go anywhere without notifying us first.'

The warning hung in the air, a thinly veiled threat that sent a chill down Robbie's spine.

'Sure. Should we contact the British Embassy or Consulate?' Robbie asked, grasping at any straw, any avenue of assistance or support.

'No need for that. We'll do that. The best thing you can do is ensure we are kept fully informed of everything, then go about enjoying the rest of your holiday. The fewer people you mention this to, the better.'

The officer's words felt like a dismissal, a brush-off that left Robbie and Scott reeling with confusion and anger.

'Really? Wouldn't it be good if we told everyone, tried to get it on the news, and put up posters? I would have thought it was important that as many people as possible knew,' Scott argued, his frustration boiling over.

'No. Not at this stage. Not until we know why she's missing. We don't want to put her in any danger.'

The officer's words were final, a clear indication that the conversation was over and that their input was no longer welcome.

'Sure. OK. Will you let us know as soon as you hear anything?' Robbie asked, his voice small and defeated.

'Of course.' The officer's tone was insincere, a hollow promise that rang false in the oppressive silence of the room.

'What now?' said Scott as they stood on the pavement outside the police station, the bright sunlight a jarring contrast to the dark and oppressive atmosphere of the interview room.

'I don't trust him at all. That was odd.' Robbie's words were laced with suspicion and unease. His mind raced with the implications of the officer's behaviour and the nagging sense that something was very wrong.

'Me neither, but what do we do?'

'I don't know. Come on, let's go back,' Robbie said, his tone determined and resolute.

'Go back where?' Scott asked, confusion and uncertainty etched on his face.

'To Cara's place? I don't want to leave all this in the police's hands. We know they have a reputation for being corrupt and inefficient. There's something odd going on and I can't put my finger on what it is.

'You know - my grandma always used to say, when things seemed odd - 'it smells a funny colour' - that's what I think about this. Something's not right.'

Robbie's words hung in the air, a dark cloud of suspicion and unease settling over them, a shared sense of foreboding that they couldn't quite shake.

'OK—to Hotel Hibiscus it is,' Scott agreed, his jaw set with determination as they hailed a taxi and set off towards the hotel. Their minds spun with questions and fears, their hearts heavy with the knowledge that Cara's fate hung in the balance and that they were her only hope.

. . .

'Hello, who is this?' asked Rachel, her voice tight with a mix of fear and anticipation as she cradled the phone to her ear. There seemed to be an extraordinarily long pause before anyone spoke, the silence stretching out like an elastic band, ready to snap at any moment.

'Can I speak to Cara Jeffries?' The voice on the other end of the line was male, unfamiliar and distant, with an edge of authority that made Rachel's skin crawl.

'Cara's not here at the moment. Can I take a message?'

'When are you expecting her back?'

'Who is this?' Rachel demanded, her voice rising with a mix of anger and desperation.

'A friend.'

The reply was curt and evasive, a non-answer that only heightened Rachel's sense of unease.

'Which friend?' Rachel pressed, her fingers tightening around the phone.

'I'm calling from St Lucia.'

The words sent a chill down Rachel's spine, a confirmation of her worst fears, a sign that something had happened to Cara.

'Is this Tajo?'

Rachel's voice was barely above a whisper, the name of Cara's mysterious boyfriend falling from her lips like a curse.

'No. How do you know Tajo?'

The voice on the other end of the line was sharp and probing, a hint of suspicion creeping into the caller's tone.

'I don't know him. Tell me who this is, or I'm hanging up.'

Rachel's words were a bluff, a desperate attempt to gain

some control over the situation, to glean some information about Cara's whereabouts and well-being.

'I'm calling from St Lucia Police Station,' said the man, his voice cold and official. 'You need to tell me everything you know about Cara Jeffries' whereabouts. Are you expecting her back soon?'

'No, no. What do you mean - you're calling from the police? Is she OK? What's happened?' Rachel's words tumbled out in a rush, her voice rising with panic and fear.

'It's nothing to worry about, but she has gone missing, and we thought she might have headed back to the UK. When did you last speak to her?'

The officer's tone was neutral, almost bored, starkly contrasting the gravity of his words and the fear gripping Rachel's heart.

'She's gone missing? Oh my God. It will be Tajo. He stole her money. He's a complete thug. What if he hurts her? You must help.'

'I am helping. I'm phoning you as part of our enquiries. When did you last speak to her?'

Rachel called Katherine into the room, and together, they told the officer everything they knew, their voices shaking with fear and emotion as they recounted the details of Cara's last few days on the island: the stolen money, the mysterious boyfriend, the growing sense of unease that had settled over them like a dark cloud.

'We'll be in touch,' said the officer, his voice curt and dismissive.

'Can I take your name in case we need to call you?' Rachel asked in a last-ditch attempt to gain some control over the situation, to have some way of following up and ensuring that Cara's case was being taken seriously.

But the officer hung up, the dial tone echoing in Rachel's ear.

'I don't like this at all,' said Katherine, her voice trembling with emotion. 'Do you think she's OK?'

Rachel shook her head slowly, her eyes brimming with tears, her heart heavy with the weight of her own helplessness and despair. 'No, I don't think she is.'

ROBBIE AND SCOTT loitered around at the hotel entrance, waiting for someone to come past and let them through. Without a pass, there was nothing they could do. They had planned to go and find her room and look for any clues at all...anything that might help them to understand where Cara had gone, but they couldn't even get through the doors.

The sun beat down on them mercilessly; oppressive and stifling.

'Let's think about this logically,' said Scott, his brow furrowed in concentration. 'She gets a phone call. Who is the call from?'

The question hung in the air, a puzzle to be solved, a mystery to be unravelled.

'If we knew that, I suspect we'd know where she's gone,' Robbie replied, his tone heavy with sarcasm and despair.

'Do you think that was the guy who stole her money?' Scott asked, his mind racing with the possibilities, the pieces of the puzzle failing to fit together in any coherent way.

'Perhaps he phoned her and told her he had the money, so she went to see him, and he kidnapped her?' Robbie suggested.

'They could have made up, and it's all a misunderstanding, and they are spending time together?' Scott offered, grasping at straws, at any possibility that didn't involve Cara being in harm's way.

'Send them in,' said Amelia, her voice tight with a mix of curiosity and apprehension. She didn't get police officers visiting her at the hotel very often and hoped nothing serious had happened.

'How can I help you?' she asked, her tone professional and courteous, belying the unease that churned in her gut. 'You have a staff member called Cara Jeffries working here?'

The officer's voice was brusque and business-like, his eyes scanning the room with a practised gaze.

'Which department?' Amelia asked, her mind racing as she tried to place the name, to match it with a face and a role within the hotel hierarchy.

'She teaches windsurfing and sailing.'

'Ah, OK. That's a separate entity. Let me get Happy in here. He looks after that.'

Happy took a call from Amelia and dashed out of the water sports centre, opening the gate and allowing two British-looking men through. He ran up to his boss's office and knocked on the door, his heart pounding in his chest as he tried to make sense of the unexpected visit. Who on earth had gone to the police?

'Come in,' shouted Amelia, her voice muffled by the heavy wooden door.

'You wanted to see me?' Happy asked, his tone cautious

and respectful, belying the fear and uncertainty that gripped his heart.

As soon as Happy's eyes rested on the officers' faces, he looked horrified, his expression a mix of shock and recognition, a confirmation of his worst fears.

'What do you want?' he asked, his voice tight with a mix of anger and apprehension.

'Do you know Cara Jeffries?'

The officer's question was a demand, a thinly veiled accusation that hung in the air like a threat.

'She works here, teaching watersports.'

'And when did you last see her?' The officer's voice was sharp and probing, his eyes boring into Happy's with an intensity that made him want to look away.

'Her last shift. Why?' Happy's reply was curt and evasive, a non-answer that only served to heighten the officer's suspicion.

'She's gone missing. Have you seen her today?'

'I saw her this morning. She'd taken the day off and was visiting friends.'

Happy's voice was steady and calm, a practised lie that rolled off his tongue with ease

'You've not seen her since?'

'No. But I wouldn't expect to. What makes you think she's gone missing?'

Happy's words were a challenge, a desperate attempt to deflect suspicion, to buy himself some time to think, to plan his next move.

'The friends with her this morning haven't seen her since she got up and left the restaurant at 11am.' The officer's voice was cold and matter-of-fact

'Oh, right. So she's a missing person?'

Happy's question was a bluff, a calculated risk, a way to

gauge the officer's reaction and glean some information about their knowledge and suspicion. He knew the police wouldn't declare someone a missing person a few hours after they'd last been seen. There was something else at play here.

It was incredibly frustrating that her friends had gone to the police. This could all have been managed so much more smoothly without their involvement.

'We'd like to see Cara's room, please,' said the officers, their voices cold and authoritative.

'Sure, I'll show you,' said Happy, his tone deferent and accommodating, belying the panic that gripped his heart. 'You must be getting extremely worried now she's been missing all afternoon.'

The officer caught Happy's eye, and they stared at one another until the officer turned away. A silent battle of wills, a test of nerves and resolve.

'This is it,' said Happy, indicating the hut that had been occupied by Cara for the last few weeks. 'This is her base, but she can stay with friends anytime, so she might not stay here every night.'

'I'll need a list of all her friends.' The officer's demand hung in the air, a reminder of the power he held over Happy and his carefully constructed world.

'I don't have a list of all her friends. I know she lives with a group of girls in England, and they are like family to her, but I'm not sure what friends she's made since she's been here.'

'Don't worry, we've already spoken to the girls in England.'

The officer's words hit Happy like a physical blow, a confirmation of his worst fears, a sign that the situation had spiraled out of control.

'Sure,' said Happy, his voice tight with a mix of anger and frustration. The officers walked into the small hut, so brightly decorated and neatly appointed that it caught them by surprise.

Inside, Robbie and Scott sat on the bed, going through a box of Cara's things.

'Who the hell are you?' asked Happy, his voice tight with a mix of anger and apprehension.

'What are you doing here?' asked the police officers, their voices cold and authoritative.

'We just wanted to see whether we could see any clues about where she went.'

'And did you find any clues?'

'Nothing.' Scott's reply was curt and defeated, a stark contrast to the determination that blazed in his eyes.

'We'll handle this case from now on. If there's anything to report, we'll be in touch with you straight away.'

The officer's words were a dismissal, a clear indication that Robbie and Scott's presence was no longer welcome, that their input was no longer required or desired.

'Sure,' said Robbie and Scott, rising from the bed and heading towards the exit, their expressions a mix of frustration and defeat, a shared sense of helplessness and despair.

'Who are you?' asked Happy as the two men walked past him, his voice tight with a mix of anger and suspicion.

'I'm Scott and this is Robbie. We're friends of Cara's. We were with her today and reported the fact that she'd gone missing to the police. Who are you?'

'I'm Happy. I'm Cara's boss.' Happy's reply was curt and business-like.

'OK, that makes sense,' said Scott. 'I'm sure we'll see you again soon.'

Happy spent the rest of the day rushing around at the

command of the two arrogant police officers who continued to look for clues for someone who had left no clues. He ran around, checking whether her key card had been used to access the hotel or the watersports area. No, it hadn't. Was there any CCTV of her? No, there wasn't.

Two hours later, the officers left, promising to send someone back the following day to trawl CCTV footage in more detail. The thought made Happy's skin crawl, a reminder of the constant surveillance, the ever-present threat of exposure and discovery.

'We will find her,' said Officer Emanuel, his voice cold and matter-of-fact.

∼

KATHERINE PACED BACK and forth in the living room; her phone clutched tightly in her hand. She glanced at Rachel and Jools sitting on the couch, their faces etched with worry. Since the call from the police earlier that day, informing them that Cara was missing, they hadn't been able to do anything. The news had hit them like a bombshell, leaving them shocked and afraid.

'We can't sit here and do nothing,' Katherine said, her voice trembling with emotion. 'Cara's out there, God knows where, and she needs our help.'

Rachel stood up, her eyes blazing with determination. 'You're right. We need to go to St Lucia and find her ourselves.'

Jools nodded in agreement, her hands twisting nervously in her lap. 'But what about work? We can't just up and leave without notice.'

Katherine shook her head, her jaw set with resolve. 'Screw work. This is Cara we're talking about.'

The girls exchanged glances. They'd all been through so much together. They knew what they had to do, no matter the cost.

Rachel grabbed her laptop and started typing furiously. 'I'll book the tickets. The next flight out is in six hours. We need to move fast.'

Jools jumped up and ran to her room, her voice trailing behind her. 'I'll start packing.'

Katherine pulled out her phone and began dialling. 'I'll call work and let them know I'm taking a week off. It's an emergency, and they'll just have to understand.'

The next few hours passed in a blur of frenzied activity. The girls raced around the apartment, throwing clothes into suitcases, gathering essentials, and making hurried phone calls to tie up loose ends. The air was thick with tension and urgency; the knowledge that every second counted weighed heavily on their minds.

'I'm so worried,' said Katherine as they wheeled their cases out to the car. What if we never see her again?'

Rachel wrapped an arm around Katherine's shoulders, her own eyes glistening with unshed tears. 'We will see her again. We're not coming back without her.'

Jools nodded, her face set with grim determination. 'Cara's strong. She'll hold on until we get there.'

The girls piled their suitcases and bags into the boot.

'I'm getting a touch of deja vu here,' said Katherine. 'Didn't we make this journey in your car just a few weeks ago, Jools?'

'We did indeed. Honestly, once we know she's safe, I'm going to strangle that woman. The things we do for our friends.'

CHAPTER
NINETEEN

4th July

CARA JOLTED AWAKE, heart pounding, the fading echo of a snapping branch still ringing in her ears. She lay motionless on the thin, musty mattress, barely daring to breathe, straining to hear any other sound that might signal an intruder's approach. But there was only silence, broken intermittently by the mournful cry of a distant bird or the skittering of some small creature in the underbrush.

After several tense minutes, Cara finally exhaled. She sat up slowly, wincing as the rough wooden slats of the floor dug into her bare feet. Dim grey light filtered through the cracks in the shutters over the hut's sole window. It was time to venture out for the daily parcel of food that Tom would be leaving for her. Perhaps there would be a note with the food, telling her of the plans for her escape?

Cara pulled on the oversized men's jacket - her only

protection against the chill mountain air. She had to roll the sleeves up several times just to free her hands. Shuffling over to the door, she pressed an ear against it, listening hard. Silence. Ever so carefully, she slid back the bolt and eased the door open a crack, just wide enough to peer out.

The mountainside was still shrouded in deep blue shadows, the contours of the surrounding forest only hinted at by the lightening sky. Mist curled eerily between the trees. There was no sign of human presence, but Cara knew that meant nothing. They could be out there even now, watching, waiting.

She glanced in all directions again and then darted out, keeping low to the ground. The morning dew soaked through her thin shoes. Shivering, Cara crept along the faint path, heart in her throat, imagining every rustle to be the sound of pursuit. The parcel was there, nestled between the roots of a gnarled fig tree. She snatched it and sprinted back to the temporary safety of the hut.

Inside once more, Cara sagged against the door, shaking from more than cold. The parcel dropped from her numb fingers. This overwhelming terror during her brief foray outside was the same every morning, but it never got easier. Each day alone in this dark little hut, with nothing but her own increasingly desperate thoughts for company, sharpened her fear.

Still, there was always the hope that today was the day she'd be leaving. She tore open the parcel to see no key or instructions. Only a scrap of paper with seven terse words scrawled across it: 'Head to watersports beach tonight after 10.'

But where on the beach? What was this? Who would be there when she got there?

She tried to focus on the positives...she was getting out.

She needed to make sure that she ate well to build up her energy. She made herself open the rest of the parcel - some fruit, a hunk of bread, ham and cheese. She sighed, her breath misting in the dank air. What she wouldn't give for a hot cup of coffee or one of those buttery croissants from the little bakery near their apartment at home.

Nibbling disinterestedly at a mango, Cara sank onto the rickety chair beside the ancient, rust-pitted stove that hulked in the corner. She'd long since given up trying to coax any heat from it. The risk of the smoke giving away her location was too high. So she sat, shivered, and stared blankly at the cobweb-draped walls, trying not to think about how filthy she was.

Time passed, minutes crawling by with unbearable slowness, marked only by the shifting angle of the light seeping into the hut. Cara alternated between huddling in the chair and pacing back and forth over the uneven floorboards. A sudden prickling sensation made her glance down, and she recoiled at the sight of a many-legged insect skittering across her foot. With a choked cry, she shook it off violently and stumbled back, colliding painfully with the edge of the stove.

God, she wanted her normal, boring life back, with all its petty imperfections. She wanted to feel safe, clean, and warm. She wanted to laugh with her friends, flirt with cute baristas and complain about the weather. She wanted to feel human again. Evening couldn't come fast enough.

She ate a little more of the food; then she heard a sound that made her blood freeze... the unmistakable crunch of approaching footsteps. She moved towards the back of the cabin, her heart slamming against her ribs, the food forgotten. Hardly breathing, she edged against the walls, towards the window and peered through a gap in the boards. For a moment, she saw nothing. Then, a flicker of movement drew her gaze, and her stomach dropped. There, winding slowly but purposefully up the narrow track, was a man. As she watched in mute horror, he paused and looked directly at the hut. And smiled.

Cold sweat prickled along Cara's spine. They'd found her. After all her precautions and sufferings, they'd found her anyway. A scream clawed at the back of her throat, but she swallowed it down. To give in to blind panic now would mean almost certain capture or worse.

Cara made herself think. The man was alone, at least for the moment, and he was still a good distance away. If she slipped out the back way, perhaps she could lose him in the forest. It was a desperate gamble, but it was better than waiting here meekly for the end.

Her movements were jerky with terror but fueled by survival instinct. Cara snatched up the jacket and shrugged it on. Then she crept to the rear window, breath coming in shallow gasps, and unlatched it as quietly as possible. Luckily, the rotting frame gave way with only a slight creak of protest.

Cara wedged herself through the narrow gap and tumbled gracelessly to the ground on the other side. For a moment, she crouched there, chest heaving, fighting the urge to bolt mindlessly into the trees.

Haltingly at first, but with growing determination, Cara crept into the undergrowth, keeping the hut between herself and the approaching threat. Branches snagged at her clothes and hair; roots seemed to twist underfoot to trip her, but she pressed on, trying to move as silently as possible. If she could just reach the stream that cut through this part of the woods, she might be able to hide her trail...

But before she'd gone more than a dozen yards, a sharp

snap rang out behind her, followed by an unfamiliar male voice.

'Going somewhere, sweetheart?'

CHAPTER
TWENTY

Mary's story: 4th July

I TAP my pen on the table, then chew it absently while I stare at the empty notebook, my mind racing with the countless questions and uncertainties that swirl through my thoughts.

'There's so much to try and work out here. The whole thing is insane,' I say, my voice tinged with frustration and bewilderment.

Ted leans back in his chair, his gaze drifting towards the turquoise waters stretching before us. 'We could just forget all about it,' he suggests, his tone casual, almost dismissive. 'We're at a café on the seafront. The Caribbean Sea is lapping onto the soft sands beside us, and we're wasting our time trying to find someone we've never met.'

His words send a flare of anger through me, and I clench my jaw, fighting back the urge to snap at him. 'But we can't just forget it. What are we going to do with that bag, for starters?' I signal towards the large sports bag lying at our feet, the weight of its contents seeming to mock us with their presence. Ted has the handle of it wrapped around his ankle, a futile attempt at securing it as if it might sprout legs and run away at any moment.

'We could either call the police and ask them to take it, or we could put it back in the locker at the station. My preference would be for the police station,' he says, his voice infuriatingly calm, as if we're discussing nothing more consequential than the weather.

I bite down hard on the pen, the plastic cracking between my teeth as I turn to face Ted, my eyes blazing with fierce determination.

'I feel a responsibility for her, though,' I say, my voice barely above a whisper, the words heavy with the weight of the secrets and mysteries surrounding us.

I see Ted smile, a glint of amusement in his eyes, and I realise what I've done. 'I've bitten through this bloody pen, haven't I?' I ask, already knowing the answer.

'You have blue lips,' he confirms, his grin widening, and for a moment, the tension between us dissipates, replaced by a fleeting sense of levity.

'I'm just going to the ladies,' I say, standing up and making my way through the restaurant, acutely aware of the curious stares and muffled laughter that follow me, my blue-stained lips now a beacon of my own absurdity.

As I push open the door to the ladies' room, the cool air and muted lighting offer a welcome respite from the heat and chaos of the outside world. I take a deep breath, trying to centre myself, to gather my thoughts and emotions into some semblance of order.

I step into the room and wait behind three English

women who are chatting animatedly about their flight over, their voices echoing off the tiled walls and filling the small space with a cacophony of sound.

I find myself drawn into their conversation, their friendly faces and easy camaraderie a balm to my frayed nerves.

'Did you know you have bright blue pen on your face?' one of the women says.

'Oh, that's my new lipstick. It's all the rage out here in St Lucia.'

THE WOMEN LAUGH and introduce themselves as Katherine, Rachel, and Jools. They seem really nice, their smiles warm and genuine, and for a moment, I allow myself to relax, to forget about the dark cloud of uncertainty that hangs over me.

I look into the mirror and am astonished at the state of my face.

'Christ, this pen juice has got everywhere,' I say, trying to keep my tone light.

'I think it's called ink,' one of them says, her voice tinged with amusement, and I can't help but laugh, the absurdity of the situation striking me with a sudden, sharp clarity.

'What are you planning to do when you're here?' I ask. 'I couldn't help overhearing that you've just arrived.'

'Yes, we are here to find our flatmate who's gone missing.'

Then, the sickening realisation dawns on me.

'Not Cara Jeffries?' I ask.

'Yes. Do you know her?' they ask, their eyes widening with surprise and a flicker of hope.

'Oh my God. Oh my God. We're looking for her too,' I say, the words spilling out of me in a breathless rush, my heart pounding in my chest as the threads of fate appear to have weaved themselves together.

'Wow. There's quite a group of us then. I talked to two guys this morning who are coming to join us because they were the last people to see her before she disappeared.'

I lead them back to the table where Ted is waiting, my mind reeling with the implications of this unexpected encounter. The women join us, their faces etched with worry and determination, and we begin to compare notes, trying to piece together the fragments of Cara's disappearance and to make sense of the tangled web of secrets and lies that surround us.

Robbie and Scott arrive a few minutes later, their expressions grim and haunted, and they provide a few crucial details about seeing Cara act suspiciously before disappearing. They talk about her having her money stolen, and the three women nod in recognition, their own stories corroborating the tale.

Ted and I share our discoveries: the purse, the station lockers, the cryptic clues that seem to lead nowhere and everywhere.

The weight of the responsibility we've taken on settles over us like a physical burden, the knowledge that Cara's fate may rest in our hands a daunting, terrifying prospect.

Robbie and Scott mention two guys, Happy and Tom, who have been trying to help, and they suggest calling them to join our impromptu gathering. But a flicker of unease runs through me at the mention of Happy's name, a nagging doubt that won't let go. I share this fear with the others.

'I think we need to talk to him all the same,' says

Robbie, and Scott nods in agreement, so they place the call, and we wait, the tension in the air thick and palpable.

When Happy arrives, he seems astonished to see Ted and me there, his eyes widening with surprise and a flicker of something else, something darker and more difficult to read.

We tell him how worried we are, the whole sordid tale spilling out of us in a rush of words and emotions. He can't believe it when Ted and I reveal that we found the purse, his expression shifting from shock to confusion to a dawning realisation.

He says he buried it in the sand for Cara to find, but it disappeared, vanishing into thin air like a ghost in the night.

'We thought you might know that we had it because you followed us when we went to the boat party to give the purse back to Cara,' I say, my voice trembling with a mix of accusation and fear.

'Oh, is that why you went to the boat? What makes you think I was following you?' he asks, his tone defensive, almost angry.

'We saw your pickup in the back of all our pictures,' Ted explains, his voice steady and calm.

'I didn't follow you. I went to the boat because I was keeping an eye on it to see whether any of the gang who stole Cara's money were on it, but when I saw you, I decided to hang around and keep an eye on you. I was worried about your safety,' Happy says, his words ringing hollow in my ears, a flimsy excuse that does little to assuage my doubts.

'So what now? Where is she? Let's go and get her,' Scott says, his voice edged with a desperate urgency, a fierce determination that mirrors mine. But Happy is reluctant, citing the danger posed by the gang members, their weapons and their ruthless, violent nature.

'But she's been there for days. We have to get her out,' Katherine argues, her voice rising with a mix of anger and desperation.

'Where is she?' Rachel asks

'She's exactly where I took Mary and Ted that day to look at the church and the graveyards. I used that opportunity to check on her.'

Happy's words hit me like a physical blow. I'm not convinced of his innocence in all this.

'Bloody hell. Did you know we have the bag from the locker at the train station?' Ted asks, his voice heavy with a mix of disbelief and anger. Happy looks down and sees the sports bag on the floor, his expression unreadable, a mask of stone that reveals nothing of the thoughts and emotions that churn beneath the surface.

Then he shakes his head in disbelief.

'Look, we want to help,' I say, my voice soft and pleading. 'We can't get on with our honeymoon and enjoy ourselves until we know that Cara is safe. Her friends have flown out from England. Can we please not just go and get her, or call the police or do something?'

The words hang between us. The seconds tick by until finally, Happy nods, his expression grim and determined. 'Okay, let's go and get her,' he says. 'Ted, give me that bag.'

Happy wanted the weapons. This was all getting very scary.

We gather our things and set off towards church hill, our hearts pounding with fear and determination. Our minds are racing with the possibilities of what we might find and the horrors that could await us in the shadows of the church and the graveyards.

But one thought burns bright within me: we will finally meet Cara and find out exactly what happened to her.

But not yet. As we gather our belongings, pay our bills, and head out towards the cars, we have no idea of the fights that lie ahead of us.

CHAPTER
TWENTY-ONE

Robbie, Scott, and Mary stood at the foot of the steep hill, their eyes fixed on the narrow, winding path that leads to the hidden hut where Cara was believed to be. The sun beat down on their shoulders, its scorching heat a palpable presence as a light breeze rustled the leaves of the surrounding trees.

The rest of the group; Katherine, Rachel, Jools, Ted, and Tom, were already preparing to climb, checking their supplies and tightening their shoelaces. Happy stood ahead of them, his stance tense and coiled, like a predator ready to strike.

'I don't know about this,' Mary said, her voice trembling, her heart pounding in her chest as a cold sweat beaded on her brow. 'What if something goes wrong up there? What if they need help?'

Scott placed a reassuring hand on Mary's shoulder, his touch a momentary comfort amidst the rising tide of fear and uncertainty.

'They'll be fine,' he said, but the words sounded hollow, even to his own ears.

The group started trudging up the mountainside, their figures growing smaller, swallowed by the dense foliage, moving out of view.

Robbie and Scott looked at one another,

'I'm not sure about this,' said Robbie, his voice low and strained. 'I agree with Mary. I have a bad feeling. Do you think we should go too?'

'I don't know. Maybe we should call the police, just in case.'

Robbie nodded, his expression grim, his jaw clenched. 'Good idea. And maybe we should see if there's anyone else who can help, too. Like that UK police officer you mentioned who was staying at the resort—what was his name again?'

'Barney. I'll give him a call and let him know what's going on.'

As Mary dialled Barney's number, her fingers trembling, her breath coming in short, sharp gasps, Scott pulled out his phone and searched for the local police station's contact information.

The rest of the group were now out of sight, navigating the steep, uneven terrain. Their progress would be painfully slow in this searing midday heat, each step a Herculean effort.

Scott paced back and forth as he waited for the police to answer, his free hand clenched into a fist, his nails digging into his palm. Robbie and Mary watched him anxiously, their hearts pounding in their chests, a deafening drumbeat in the stillness of the clearing.

After what felt like an eternity, Scott finally spoke into the phone, his voice urgent and strained, the words tumbling out in a rush, a desperate plea for help.

'Yes, hello. We need your help. Our friend, she's missing,

and we think she's in trouble...' As Scott relayed the details of their situation to the police, his words punctuated by the static crackle of the connection, Mary's phone rang.

It was Barney.

'Mary? What's going on? You sounded worried on the phone.' Barney's voice was a soothing presence in the chaos and confusion. She updated him on the situation, her words tumbling out in a rush.

'Cara's in a hut up on the hill. Katherine and the others have gone to find her, but we're worried they might need backup. Ted's gone up there too. I'm really worried.

There was a brief pause on the other end of the line, and then Barney's strong and determined voice came through. 'I'm on my way. Stay where you are, and don't do anything reckless. I'll be there as soon as I can.'

Mary ended the call, her heart racing, her palms slick with sweat. She turned to Robbie and Scott, who huddled together, their faces etched with worry, their eyes haunted by the spectre of what might lie ahead.

'Barney's coming,' she said, her voice trembling, a quiver of fear and relief mingling in her tone.

'And the police are on their way, too,' said Scott. The three friends fell silent, their gazes fixed on the hill where their friends had disappeared; the weight of their absence felt like a physical presence.

The minutes ticked by, each feeling like an eternity.

Suddenly, sirens pierced the air, growing louder as they approached, their wailing cry a herald of hope. Two police cars screeched to a halt at the base of the hill, and four officers emerged, their faces grim and determined, their movements sharp and precise, a choreography of purpose and intent.

Scott rushed over to them, his words coming out in a

jumble as he tried to explain the situation, his voice raw with emotion, his eyes wild with fear.

'Please, you have to help them! Our friends have gone up there to save Cara, but we don't know what they're walking into...'

The words caught in his throat, a choking sob that threatened to tear him apart from the inside out.

The officers nodded, their hands resting on their weapons, their eyes hard and unreadable.

They quickly conferred, then turned to Scott, Robbie, and Mary, their expressions inscrutable, their words clipped and precise.

'We'll take it from here,' one of them said, his voice firm, a command that brooked no argument. 'You three stay put. We'll make sure your friends are safe.'

With that, the officers began to climb the hill, their movements swift and purposeful, their figures quickly swallowed by the dense foliage, disappearing from view like ghosts in the mist.

Robbie, Scott, and Mary watched as they disappeared, vanished into the dense foliage, their hearts in their throats, their minds reeling with the possibilities of what might lie ahead.

Next to arrive was Barney, his face flushed and his breathing heavy, his chest heaving with exertion and urgency.

'Where are they?' Barney demanded, his eyes scanning the hillside, his gaze sharp and penetrating, a hunter seeking his prey.

Mary pointed up the path, her hand shaking, her fingers trembling with a mix of fear and exhaustion. 'They went up there, all of them. The police just left, too.'

Barney nodded, his jaw clenched, his expression a mask

of determination and resolve. 'Right. I will go after them. You three stay here and wait for news.'

Without another word, Barney began to climb...his determination evident in every step, his movements fluid and graceful, a predator on the hunt.

Robbie, Scott, and Mary huddled together, their eyes fixed on the spot where their friends had vanished, praying they would all return safely.

∼

As the group neared the top of the hill, the hut came into view, a dilapidated structure of weathered wood and rusted metal, its windows dark and foreboding. The air was thick with tension, a palpable sense of unease settled over them like a shroud. They approached cautiously, their footsteps muffled by the soft earth, their breaths coming in short, sharp gasps.

Katherine reached the door first, her hand trembling as she reached for the handle, the metal cold and unyielding beneath her fingers. She hesitated, her heart pounding in her chest, her mind reeling with the possibilities of what might lie beyond. But then, with a deep breath and a silent prayer, she pushed the door open, the hinges creaking in protest, the sound a deafening roar in the stillness of the clearing.

The scene that greeted them was one of horror and despair. Cara sat in the centre of the room, her arms and legs bound to a chair, her mouth gagged with a dirty rag. Her eyes were wide with fear, her face streaked with tears and grime, her body trembling with exhaustion and terror. The group rushed forward, their hearts in their throats, their minds numb with shock and disbelief.

But before they could reach her, two figures emerged from the shadows, their faces twisted with malice, their eyes glinting with a cruel, predatory light. Their arms were outstretched, guns pointed directly at the group's chests. The air was electric with tension, a crackling energy that threatened to explode at any moment.

Ted and Happy reacted instantly, their bodies moving on instinct, their minds focused on a single, overwhelming imperative: to protect Cara at all costs. They lunged forward, their hands outstretched, their eyes blazing with a fierce, primal rage. They grappled with the gang members, their bodies straining with the effort, their muscles screaming in protest.

For a moment, it seemed as though they might prevail, their strength and determination a match for the gang members' brute force and cruelty. But then, just as they had the men pinned to the ground, their arms twisted behind their backs, their faces pressed into the dirt, a new threat emerged from the shadows.

The police officers who had arrived on the scene were not the saviours they had hoped for, but rather corrupt members of the gang, their loyalty bought and paid for with blood money and promises of power. They turned their guns on Ted and Happy, their eyes cold and merciless, their fingers hovering over the triggers.

Cara thrashed in her chair, her muffled screams a wordless plea for help, her eyes wide with terror and desperation. The sound of the guns cocking was like a death knell, a final, terrible pronouncement of their fate.

Barney arrived on the scene when it looked like all hope was lost. He waited outside the hut, looking in. His presence a secret weapon, a last, desperate hope in the face of overwhelming odds. He caught Tom's eye, a silent communication passing between them, a shared understanding of what needed to be done.

Together, they rushed forward, their movements a blur of speed and agility, their bodies fuelled by adrenaline and desperation. Barney threw himself at one of the gunmen, his fist connecting with the man's jaw with a sickening crack, the force of the blow sending him sprawling to the ground. Tom grappled with the other, his hands searching for the gun, his fingers closing around the cold metal with a grip of iron.

Katherine, Rachel, and Jools sprang into action, their own safety forgotten in the face of their friend's peril. They lunged for the remaining gang members, their hands clawing at their faces, their feet kicking at their shins, their voices raised in a chorus of rage and defiance.

The sound of sirens filled the air, a distant promise of hope and salvation, as Barney's reinforcements arrived on the scene, a squadron of officers he knew to be honest and true. They swarmed the hut, their weapons drawn, their eyes hard and determined, their voices raised in a shout of command and authority.

In the chaos and confusion, Cara was freed from her bonds, her body collapsing into the arms of her friends, her sobs of relief and gratitude mingling with their own tears of joy and exhaustion. They clung to each other, their hearts beating as one, their minds reeling with the realisation of how close they had come to losing everything.

As the gang members were led away in handcuffs, their faces sullen and defeated, their eyes filled with a dull, impotent rage, Cara turned to Tom, her eyes shining with a love and gratitude that words could never express. She buried her face in his chest, her tears soaking his shirt, her body shaking with the force of her emotions.

CHAPTER
TWENTY-TWO

The sun hung low in the sky, casting a warm, orange glow over the hill as the group descended, their faces a mix of relief and exhaustion. Katherine and Rachel supported Cara between them, her steps faltering but her spirit unbroken. Jules followed close behind, her eyes darting between her friend and the police officers who escorted the criminals down the narrow path.

At the base of the hill, Cara was whisked away to the hospital, accompanied by Tom, Robbie, and Scott. Their voices were low and soothing as they assured her that everything would be alright, that she was safe now.

As the ambulance pulled away, sirens blaring, Happy motioned for Mary and Ted to join him under the shade of a nearby tree. They sat in the cool grass, their backs against the rough bark, as Happy began to speak.

'There's something you need to know,' he said, his voice heavy with the weight of the truth. 'About Cara, and what really happened.'

Mary and Ted leaned in, their eyes wide with curiosity and concern.

Happy took a deep breath, his gaze fixed on the horizon.

'Cara's aunt passed away recently,' he began, his voice soft. 'She left Cara a lot of money—over £100,000.'

Mary gasped, her hand flying to her mouth. Ted's brow furrowed, his mind racing with questions.

'One of the local gang members, he befriended Cara,' Happy continued, his eyes darkening. 'Convinced her to invest in some scheme, promised her millions in return.'

He shook his head, a bitter smile tugging at his lips. 'Of course, it was all a lie. They took her money, every last penny. Left her with nothing.

'Cara came to me and asked for help,' Happy said, his voice growing stronger. Once I worked out that the guys who had stolen her money were from the Lyon gang, I realised I could help. I knew someone who had a huge influence over the Lyons. He lived in Jamaica and owed me a favour, so I contacted him and got him to intervene.'

He paused, his gaze flickering at Mary and Ted. 'I got Cara's money back. But we knew she wasn't safe. We knew that once the gang realised what had happened, they would come after her.'

Mary's eyes widened, realisation dawning. 'That's why you took her up the hill,' she breathed. 'To hide her.'

Happy nodded, a small smile tugging at his lips. 'I've been visiting her daily, bringing food and leaving notes. We planned to keep her safe until she could leave the country.'

'Right. That makes sense.'

'When it came time for her to leave, I buried a load of money in the sand, along with the details of a boat party the following night. The idea was for Cara to slip away while the gang was distracted at the party. There was enough cash for her to buy a ticket and deal with any problems that might come up.'

Ted's face paled, realisation hitting him like a ton of bricks. 'The purse,' he whispered, his voice hoarse. 'The one we found buried in the sand. We thought it was someone's lost property, we had no idea...'

Happy sighed, running a hand over his face. 'When you found that purse, it threw everything into chaos. Cara panicked, thought the gang had found her. She rummaged on the beach for so long, looking for it, that she was seen - they found her. That's why they were able to get hold of her here.

'It was me who dug the beach up. We have a small digger at the hotel – I took it onto the beach and dug everything up, looking for the purse.'

The three of them sat in silence, each lost in their own thoughts. The truth of Cara's story hung heavy in the air, a reminder of the darkness lurking in paradise's shadows.

'And what about Tajo?

'He's a gang member. His dad was the head of the gang. It was only natural that Tajo would get involved.'

'There's something that confuses me; why did the hotel not tell anyone what was happening?' Mary asked, her voice tinged with frustration. 'Surely someone must have noticed Cara was missing. Why were there no posters up? Why wasn't anyone looking for her?'

Happy sighed, his shoulders slumping. 'No one knew she was missing for a while,' he explained, his voice low. 'Because I kept it quiet. I didn't want to draw attention to the situation. I wanted to hide her away for a couple of days and fly her out of the country when no one was looking.'

Ted nodded, his mind racing with questions. 'What about that time you ran off when the police arrived at the resort? Just after we arrived,' he asked, his eyes narrowing. 'You looked like you were trying to avoid them.'

Happy shifted uncomfortably, his gaze dropping to the ground. 'I didn't want to answer questions about the beach being dug up,' he admitted, his voice barely above a whisper. 'I was scared of revealing too much, of putting Cara in even more danger.'

Mary's eyes widened, a sudden realisation hitting her.

'Sabina lied to us on the coach,' she said, her voice trembling with anger. 'She said the story Barney had heard about there being a missing person was untrue.'

Happy held up a hand, his expression softening. 'To be fair to Sabina, she didn't know what was going on officially,' he said, his tone gentle. 'She was just trying to keep everyone calm, to prevent panic from spreading.'

Mary nodded, her anger fading as quickly as it had come. She knew Sabina had been in a difficult position, caught between the need for secrecy and the desire to keep her guests safe.

Ted's face grew serious, his eyes scanning the surrounding area as if searching for hidden threats. 'What about the rest of the gang?' he asked, his voice tight with worry. 'Are we still in danger?'

Happy shook his head, a small smile tugging at his lips. 'No, they'll be long gone,' he said, his voice firm with certainty. 'Off the island, probably halfway across the Caribbean by now. This place is useless to them without corrupt police to protect them.'

Ted nodded, relief washing over him like a cool breeze. He knew Happy was right—the gang had no reason to stay, not now that their network of corruption had been exposed and dismantled.

Mary reached out, placing a hand on Happy's arm. 'You've been incredible, she said, her voice soft with gratitude. 'We thought you were in on the whole thing, and now I feel guilty. You were the good guy in all this.'

Ted clapped Happy on the shoulder, his smile wide and genuine. 'You're a good man, Happy,' he said, his voice gruff with emotion.

'Thank you. Do you have any more questions? I know this has all been very strange and not at all what you'd expect on your honeymoon.'

'Hey, I was arrested on my hen weekend. I'm used to this sort of thing happening,' said Mary.

Happy laughed. 'Really?'

'Yes. We were dressed as nuns, got drunk and flashed people in a very religious country. You know what it's like.'

'Not really...' said Happy.

'Actually, I do have one other question - when you were visiting Cara and leaving her food and notes, did anyone ever see you? Did you have to take any special precautions to avoid being followed?'

A wry smile tugged at Happy's lips. 'I've learned a thing or two about staying under the radar,' he said, a hint of mischief in his eyes. 'I took different routes every time, never stayed too long, and always made sure I wasn't being watched. It was a risk, but it was worth it to keep Cara safe.'

Ted's face grew thoughtful, his mind turning over the pieces of the puzzle. 'The police officers who turned out to be corrupt,' he mused, his words careful and precise. 'Did you have any idea about them before all of this happened? Had you ever seen or heard anything suspicious?'

'I had my suspicions,' he admitted. 'I know a lot of people, and I've been around a lot. There are lots of great police officers, but too many bad ones for me to really trust them.'

Ted's face hardened with determination, his eyes

blazing with a fierce protectiveness. 'Now that the corrupt police have been arrested,' he said, his words sharp and unyielding, 'will there be any kind of investigation into the extent of the corruption?'

Happy sighed, his shoulders slumping with the weight of the question. 'I hope so,' he said, his voice tinged with a mix of exhaustion and determination. 'But it won't be easy. Corruption like that, it runs deep. It'll take time to root it all out.'

Mary felt a sudden rush of affection for the man sitting beside her. She reached out and placed a hand on his arm, feeling the warmth of his skin beneath her fingers.

Ted leaned forward, his elbows resting on his knees as he fixed Happy with a serious gaze. 'What about Tajo?' he asked, his voice tight with anger. 'The man who started this whole mess, who pretended to be Cara's boyfriend and led her straight into the hands of those criminals. Please tell me he won't get away with it.'

Happy's lips twisted into a grim smile, his eyes hardening with a fierce determination. 'Oh, he won't,' he said, his voice low and dangerous. 'Believe me, Tajo's getting exactly what he deserves.'

Mary shuddered, hugging her arms around herself as if to ward off a chill. 'I can't imagine how Cara must have felt,' she said softly. 'To be betrayed like that by someone she thought she could trust...'

Happy reached out, placing a comforting hand on Mary's shoulder. 'It's not going to be easy for her,' he said gently. 'Tajo's betrayal, the trauma of everything she's been through... it's going to take time for her to heal.'

He squeezed Mary's shoulder, his touch warm and reassuring. 'But she's got us,' he said firmly.

Happy's eyes glinted with a hard, unyielding light. 'And

I have the pleasure of watching what happens to Tajo now. I'll make sure things are difficult. I've got contacts who can ensure that Tajo never sees the light of day again.'

He paused, his gaze sweeping over Mary and Ted as if gauging their reactions. 'I know it's not pretty,' he said quietly. 'I know it's not the 'right' way to do things. But after what he did to Cara... I can't let him get away with it. I won't.'

Mary met Happy's gaze, her own eyes shining with understanding. 'We know,' she said softly. 'And we trust you, Happy. We know you'll do whatever it takes to keep Cara safe, to make sure justice is served.'

CHAPTER
TWENTY-THREE

I was just drifting off to sleep when my phone buzzed on the nightstand. I groaned, rolling over and fumbling for the device, my eyes still heavy with exhaustion.

'Hello?' I mumbled, my voice thick and groggy.

'Mary!' Katherine's voice was bright and chipper, far too energetic for such an early hour. 'I'm sorry to wake you, but I have wonderful news!'

I sat up, rubbing the sleep from my eyes. 'What is it?' I asked, trying to muster some enthusiasm.

'It's Cara. She's doing so much better. The doctors say she's well enough to travel, and she's coming back to England with us tomorrow morning!'

I felt a grin spread across my face, the last vestiges of sleep falling away instantly. 'That's fantastic!' I exclaimed, reaching over to shake Ted awake. 'I'm so glad to hear it.'

Katherine laughed, the sound warm and joyful. 'We're all thrilled,' she said. 'And we want to celebrate. We're having farewell drinks this evening, and we'd love for you and Ted to join us.'

I glanced at Ted, who was blinking at me with bleary eyes. 'We wouldn't miss it for the world,' I said, my heart swelling with happiness. 'What time and where?'

After jotting down the details, I ended the call and turned to Ted, my face alight with excitement. 'Cara's out of hospital today and going home tomorrow,' I said. 'She's going to be okay.'

Ted sat up, a slow smile spreading across his face. 'That's the best news I've heard in a long time,' he said, pulling me into a tight hug. 'Now – how abou us? Shall we actually get out there and see some of this island?'

I stepped out of the resort hand in hand with Ted, my face glowing with excitement as we prepared to embark on a day of adventure and relaxation.

Amelia, the resort manager, had arranged a special itinerary for us, eager to make up for the stress and chaos of the past few days. She had pulled out all the stops, determined to give us the honeymoon of our dreams.

As we settled into the plush seats of the car, I couldn't contain my grin. 'I can't believe we're actually doing this,' I said, my voice giddy with anticipation. 'A real honeymoon, just the two of us.'

Ted squeezed my hand, his own smile just as wide. 'And what a place to do it,' he said, gesturing out the window at the lush, green landscape that whizzed by. 'St. Lucia is like something out of a dream.'

Our first stop was the Sulphur Springs, a natural wonder located in the heart of the island. As we approached the site, the pungent smell of sulphur filled the air, a reminder of the volcanic activity that had shaped the island over millions of years.

We made our way to the mud baths, where a guide greeted us with a warm smile. 'Welcome,' he said, his voice rich and melodic. 'Are you ready to experience the healing powers of the mud?'

Ted and I exchanged a glance, our eyes sparkling with mischief. 'Absolutely,' we said in unison, before stripping down to our swimsuits and lowering ourselves into the warm, gooey mud.

The sensation was unlike anything I had ever experienced. The mud was soft and silky against my skin, and I could feel the heat seeping into my muscles, relaxing me from head to toe.

We spent nearly an hour soaking in the baths, laughing and splashing each other like children. When we finally emerged, my skin was smooth and glowing, and I felt like a new person.

Next on the agenda was a hike to the top of the Soufriere Volcano. The trail was steep and rocky, but the views were worth every step. As we climbed higher and higher, the island spread out before us like a lush, green carpet, the waters of the Caribbean sparkling in the distance.

At the summit, we paused to catch our breath and take in the panorama. I leaned against Ted, my head on his shoulder, and he wrapped his arm around my waist.

'This is perfect,' I murmured, my voice soft and content. 'I never want this moment to end.'

But end it did, as Amelia had even more adventures in store for us. We made our way back down the mountain and hopped into a waiting boat, ready to explore the island from a different perspective.

The boat took us to a secluded cove, where crystal-clear waters lapped at pristine white sands. We donned our snorkelling gear and dived in, marvelling at the vibrant colours of the coral reefs and the schools of tropical fish that darted past.

We spent hours exploring the underwater world, giddy with excitement as we pointed out sea turtles and stingrays to each other. When we finally surfaced, I was sun-kissed and salt-streaked but blissfully happy.

As the sun began to set, we returned to the boat, where a mouth-watering spread of local delicacies awaited us. Grilled lobster, jerk chicken, and fresh fruit adorned the table, and we dug in with gusto, washing it all down with ice-cold beers and fruity cocktails.

We ate, drank, and laughed until our bellies were full and our cheeks ached from smiling. As the stars began to twinkle overhead, Ted pulled me close and pressed a tender kiss to my lips.

'I love you,' he murmured, his voice rough with emotion. 'More than anything in this world.'

I smiled up at him, my eyes shining with tears of joy. 'I love you too,' I whispered. 'Forever and always.'

As the sun began to set, we returned to the resort to prepare for Cara's farewell drinks. I slipped into a flowy sundress and Ted donned a crisp linen shirt, and we set off hand in hand, our hearts full of joy and anticipation.

The bar was crowded with Cara's friends and family, all of them eager to celebrate her recovery and impending return home. Ted and I were greeted with hugs and kisses, and we soon found ourselves swept up in the festive atmosphere.

Cara was there, looking tired but happy, her face glowing with a newfound sense of peace and purpose. She hugged me tightly, tears glistening in her eyes as she thanked us for our support and friendship.

As the night wore on, the drinks flowed freely, and the laughter grew louder. We toasted Cara's health, the power of friendship, and the incredible adventure we had all shared.

CHAPTER
TWENTY-FOUR

The morning sun cast a warm glow over the lush gardens of the governor's mansion as Ted and I made our way up the winding path. The air was heavy with the scent of tropical flowers.

We had been invited to attend a special ceremony, one that had been hastily arranged in the wake of the dramatic events of the past few days. I smoothed my hand over the skirt of my sundress, feeling a flutter of nerves in my stomach.

As we approached the mansion, I caught sight of a familiar figure standing near the entrance. It was Happy, looking resplendent in a crisp white shirt and pressed slacks. He smiled as we drew near, his eyes crinkling at the corners.

'Mary, Ted,' he said warmly, clasping our hands in turn. 'I'm so glad you could make it.'

'We wouldn't have missed it for the world,' I said, feeling a swell of pride in my chest. 'What you did for Cara was nothing short of heroic.'

Happy ducked his head, looking suddenly bashful. 'I

only did what anyone would have done,' he said, but I could see the gleam of satisfaction in his eyes.

We followed him into the mansion, where a small crowd had gathered in the grand foyer. I recognised many of the faces - Katherine and Jools, their arms linked as they chattered excitedly; and Tom, standing tall and proud in his newly purchased suit.

But there were other people I didn't recognise - dignitaries and officials, all dressed in their finest attire. I felt a sudden rush of nerves, wondering if we were underdressed for such an occasion.

As if sensing my unease, Ted gave my hand a reassuring squeeze. 'You look beautiful,' he murmured, his eyes soft with love.

I smiled, feeling a surge of gratitude for his steady presence at my side. Together, we made our way to the front of the room, where a small stage had been set up.

The governor himself stepped up to the podium, his face solemn but his eyes warm with admiration. 'Ladies and gentlemen,' he began, his voice ringing out clear and strong. 'We are gathered here today to honour a true hero, a man who risked everything to bring justice and safety to our island.'

A hush fell over the room as all eyes turned to Happy, who stood tall and proud, his head held high. The governor beckoned him forward, and he stepped up to the stage, his movements steady and sure.

'Harold 'Happy' Matthews,' the governor continued, his voice filled with reverence. 'For your bravery, selflessness, and unwavering commitment to the truth, we would like to present you with the Order of Saint Lucia, the highest civilian honour our nation can bestow. But it won't be me doing the presentation, we have someone very special here to present it.'

All eyes turned to the door at the back of the room which opened slowly, allowing Darren Sammy to walk in. The St Lucia cricketer who Happy adored.

A gasp rippled through the crowd as Darren Sammy lifted a gleaming medal from a velvet cushion, its surface catching the light and glinting like a star. He placed it around Happy's neck, the deep, rich blue ribbon against the white of his shirt.

Happy's eyes glistened with tears as he lifted his hand to touch the medal, his fingers trembling slightly. 'Thank you,' he said, his voice thick with emotion. 'I am deeply honoured and humbled by this recognition and I'm trying not to scream and faint at the sight of Darren Sammy.'

The governor stepped back onto the stage.

'I want to tell you a little bit about Harold,' he said. 'This man grew up in a small, tight-knit community in St. Lucia. His parents worked hard to provide for their family, instilling in Happy a strong work ethic and a deep sense of loyalty to those he cared about. As a young man, Happy discovered his passion for the ocean and watersports, spending every spare moment on the beach or in the water.

'When he lost his father at a young age, he stepped up and supported his mother and younger siblings. I remember seeing this young boy become a man.

'His love for his community and his natural leadership skills have served him well, but never more than these past few days. Well done, Happy.'

'But I did not act alone,' Happy said, his voice growing stronger with each word. 'I had the help and support of some of the bravest, most compassionate people I have ever known.'

He gestured to Cara, who stood with her head held high, her eyes shining with pride. 'Cara, your strength and resilience in the face of unimaginable adversity is an inspiration to us all. You are a true survivor, and I am honoured to call you my friend.'

Cara's eyes filled with tears as she mouthed a silent 'thank you,' her hand clutching at her heart.

Happy turned next to Tom, who stood to one side, his face a mask of professionalism. 'Tom,' he said, his voice filled with respect. 'Thank you for your bravery. You aren't a St Lucian, so don't qualify for one of these medals, but please remember that this is as much yours as mine.'

Tom nodded, his jaw tight with emotion, as a ripple of applause swept through the crowd.

As the sun dipped below the horizon, Cara and her friends left the ceremony to prepare themselves for their departure.

The others gathered on the terrace of the resort, glasses clinking together in a toast to friendship, love, and the unbreakable bonds that had brought everyone together.

Tom sat beside me, his eyes distant as he swirled the ice in his glass. 'I will miss her,' he said softly, his voice barely audible above the gentle lapping of the waves against the shore. 'Cara, I mean. I know we didn't have much time together, but those moments we shared, trying to teach kids to sail, and watching them fall into the water... it brought us closer in a way I never could have imagined.'

I reached out to lay a hand on his arm, feeling the warmth of his skin beneath my fingers. 'I bet she misses you too,' I said, my voice gentle but firm.

Tom's gaze lifted to meet mine, a flicker of hope

sparking in their depths. 'You think so?' he asked, his voice hesitant, as if afraid to believe.

'I know so,' I said, my conviction unwavering. 'And that's why you have to come back with us, Tom. Come back to England, to Cara. She would be so thrilled to see you, to have you by her side.'

Tom's brow furrowed, uncertainty clouding his features. 'But my job, my life here...' he began, but I cut him off with a wave of my hand.

'None of that matters,' I said. 'What matters is love, Tom. The love you and Cara share, the love that brought you together in the first place. You can't let that slip away, not now, not after everything you've been through.'

Ted leaned forward, his eyes sparkling with mischief.

'I could think of it as an adventure,' he said, his grin infectious.

'Yes - a chance to start fresh, to build a new life with the woman you love. And who knows? Maybe you'll find your calling in England.'

Tom's lips twitched into a smile. 'An adventure, huh?' he mused, his gaze turning inward. 'I like the sound of that.'

'Then it's settled,' I said, clapping my hands together in delight. 'You're coming back with us, Tom. Book your ticket first thing in the morning, and by this time tomorrow, you'll be on a plane to England, to Cara.'

Tom's smile widened, his eyes shining with a newfound sense of hope and purpose. 'I can't believe I'm doing this,' he said, shaking his head in wonder. 'But you're right, Mary. I can't let this chance slip away. I have to take a leap of faith'

We clinked our glasses together once more, toasting new beginnings and the power of love to conquer all. As the stars began to twinkle overhead and the warm breeze carried the scent of tropical flowers, I felt a sense of deep contentment settle over me.

THE NEXT MORNING dawned bright and clear, the sun casting a golden glow over the island as we made our way to the airport. Tom's bag was packed, his ticket clutched tightly in his hand as he walked beside us, his step light and his heart full of hope.

We boarded the plane together, settling into our seats as the engines roared to life. And as we lifted off, soaring high above the turquoise waters of the Caribbean, I felt a sense of deep gratitude wash over me.

Gratitude for the love that brought us all together, for the strength and resilience that carried us through the darkest of times, for the friendships that had been forged in the crucible of adversity, for the bonds that would last a lifetime.

And most of all, gratitude for the man beside me, the one who had stood by my side through it all, the one who had loved me fiercely and without reservation. Ted, my rock, my anchor, my everything.

As the plane carried us ever closer to England, to home and to Cara, I reached out to take Ted's hand in mine, feeling the warmth and strength of his touch.

CHAPTER
TWENTY-FIVE

As the plane touched down at Heathrow Airport, I felt a wave of excitement wash over me. Ted and Tom were already gathering their belongings, their faces alight with anticipation.

We made our way through the bustling terminal, navigating the crowds of travellers and the maze of corridors until we finally emerged into the bright sunlight of the arrivals hall. There, we were greeted by the sight of a familiar face, holding a sign with our names scrawled across it in bold, black letters.

'Rachel!' I cried, rushing forward to embrace her. 'What are you doing here?'

Rachel grinned, her eyes sparkling with mischief. 'I couldn't miss the big reunion, could I?' she said, hugging me tightly. 'Besides, someone had to make sure Cara was ready for your arrival.'

I pulled back, my brow furrowed in confusion. 'Ready? What do you mean?'

Rachel's grin widened. 'Oh, you'll see,' she said cryptically.

'But first, we need to get you lot on a train to Birmingham. Cara's waiting, even if she doesn't know it yet.'

We followed Rachel to the train station, our luggage trailing behind us as we navigated the crowded platforms. And as we settled into our seats, the train pulling away from the station with a gentle lurch.

Beside me, Tom fidgeted in his seat, his hands twisting together in his lap. 'Do you think she'll be happy to see me?' he asked, his voice barely audible above the train's rumble.

I reached out to lay a hand on his arm, my eyes soft with understanding. 'Of course she will,' I said gently. 'She loves you, Tom. And you love her. That's all that matters.'

Tom nodded, a small smile playing at the corners of his lips. 'I know,' he said softly. 'I just... I can't believe this is really happening. That I'm really here, on my way to see her.'

Meanwhile, back in Birmingham, Cara was blissfully unaware of the surprise that awaited her. She had spent the morning lounging in her pyjamas, her hair a tousled mess and her face free of makeup.

But as the hours ticked by, her friends grew increasingly insistent that she get dressed and make herself presentable.

'Come on, Cara,' Katherine cajoled, pulling her friend towards the bedroom. 'You can't spend all day in your PJs. Let's get you dressed up, make you feel like a million bucks.'

Cara grumbled, but allowed herself to be led towards the wardrobe. 'I don't see why it matters,' she muttered, rifling through her clothes. 'It's not like I'm going anywhere.'

But Katherine just smiled, a knowing glint in her eye. 'Trust me,' she said, pulling out a stunning dress in a deep shade of blue. 'You're going to want to look your best today.'

As Cara slipped into the dress, the soft fabric clinging to her curves in all the right places, she had to admit that Katherine was right. She did feel better, more confident and put-together than she had in days.

She allowed her friends to fuss over her, styling her hair and applying a touch of makeup until she was practically glowing. And as she stood before the mirror, taking in her reflection, she felt a flicker of something she hadn't felt in a long time: hope.

BACK ON THE TRAIN, I watched the countryside whizz by outside the window, my thoughts drifting to Cara and the surprise that awaited her. I couldn't wait to see the look on her face when she saw Tom, to witness the joy and love that would surely radiate from every pore.

Ted reached over to take my hand in his, his fingers lacing through mine. 'She's going to be so happy,' he murmured, his eyes soft with affection. 'You did a good thing, Mary. Bringing Tom here, giving them this chance.'

I leaned my head against his shoulder, feeling the warmth of his body seep into mine. 'I just want her to be happy,' I said softly. 'After everything she's been through, she deserves it.'

As the train pulled into Birmingham station, we gathered our things and made our way out into the bustling city streets. Rachel guided us through the winding roads until we finally arrived at Cara's house.

I felt a flutter of nerves in my stomach as we approached the door, my hand trembling slightly as I reached out to knock. But before I could make contact, the door swung open, revealing a beaming Katherine on the other side.

'You're here!' she cried, ushering us inside. 'Come in, come in. Cara's in the living room, she has no idea.'

We followed Katherine down the hallway, our footsteps muffled by the plush carpet. And as we rounded the corner into the living room, I heard a gasp of surprise from the other side of the room.

There, standing before us, was Cara. She was stunning, her hair falling in soft waves around her shoulders and her eyes wide with shock. Looking equally stunned, was Tom.

For a moment, the room was silent, the air thick with tension and anticipation. And then, as if in slow motion, Cara and Tom moved towards each other, their arms outstretched and their eyes locked on each other.

They collided in the middle of the room, their bodies crashing together in a fierce embrace. Cara buried her face in Tom's chest, her shoulders shaking with sobs of joy and relief. And Tom held her close, his arms wrapped tightly around her as if he never wanted to let go.

Around them, the rest of us watched with tears in our eyes, our hearts full to bursting with happiness and love. Katherine and Rachel joined the embrace, their arms wrapping around Cara and Tom until they were all tangled together in a knot of limbs and laughter.

As the tears subsided and the laughter died down, Cara pulled back from Tom's embrace, her eyes shining with love and gratitude. 'I can't believe you're really here,' she whispered, her voice trembling with emotion.

Tom smiled, his hand reaching up to cup her cheek. 'I couldn't stay away,' he said softly. 'Not when I knew that you were waiting for me.'

Cara's eyes fluttered closed, a single tear slipping down her cheek. 'I think I might love you,' she murmured, her voice barely audible. '

Tom leaned in, his lips brushing against hers in a kiss so tender and so sweet that it made my heart ache. 'I think I might love you too,' he whispered.

CHAPTER
TWENTY-SIX

Birmingham:

As Cara settled back into her life in the UK, the memories of her tumultuous summer in St. Lucia slowly began to fade. She was starting to feel like herself again, surrounded by the love and support of her friends and family.

One evening, as she was curled up on the couch with a cup of tea, her phone rang. She glanced at the screen, surprised to see an unfamiliar number with a St. Lucian area code.

'Hello?' she answered tentatively.

'Ms. Jeffries? This is Detective Inspector James from the Royal St. Lucia Police Force. I hope I'm not catching you at a bad time.'

Cara sat up straight, her heart pounding in her chest. 'No, not at all. What can I do for you, Inspector?'

Tom looked up from his position in the armchair opposite and signalled for Cara to put the phone on the loudspeaker.

'I wanted to give you an update on our investigation

into Tajo and the gang that stole your money. We've had a major breakthrough in the case.'

Cara's eyes widened. 'Really? What happened?'

'We've had Tajo in custody for the past 48 hours. After a thorough interrogation, he confessed to his involvement in the theft of your money, as well as several other similar crimes.'

Tom jumped up and punched the air. Cara felt a wave of relief wash over her, followed quickly by a pang of betrayal.

'I can't believe it. I thought he was my friend.'

'I'm afraid that's how he operates, Ms. Jeffries. He befriends vulnerable tourists, gains their trust, and then introduces them to his gang. They steal their money and valuables, and then disappear without a trace.'

Cara shook her head, feeling foolish for having fallen for his act. 'I had no idea.'

'Please don't blame yourself. Tajo is a master manipulator. He's been doing this for years, and he's very good at what he does.

'He has left a note with us for us to send to you, if you'd like us to. We would need to read it first, but we could then send it to you.'

'Can you read it to me? I don't particularly want a letter from him, but I'd like to know what it says.'

There's the sound of shuffling papers, then a short silence.

'OK, yes. I can read this. Would you like me to read it now?'

'Yes, please.'

Dear Cara, I am sorry for everything. You are a lovely person, and I have, genuine feelings for you. If my life were simpler, I'd be with you now. But it's not.

'I told you all about my childhood once. I mentioned

my dad never being there. This is because he was in and out of jail. He was part of a gang.

I'm with that same gang now. I don't expect you to understand – but I had no choice but to do what I did. I had to choose between my loyalty to the gang and my growing love for you.

I had no choice. Please forgive me. Tajo.

'Thanks. Just throw it away,' said Cara. She didn't want to deal with the maelstrom of emotions the letter had thrown up. 'And what happens next?'

'Well, we raided Tajo's apartment in Laventille earlier today. We found a large number of stolen items, as well as a significant amount of cash, drugs, and illegal firearms.

'With the evidence we've collected and Tajo's confession, we have a very strong case against him. He's looking at a lengthy prison sentence, as well as charges for his involvement in the drug trade and illegal weapons possession.'

'I'm very grateful to you for calling. I appreciate you keeping me updated on the case.'

'Of course. We'll keep you informed of any further developments. In the meantime, please don't hesitate to reach out if you need anything. We're here to support you in any way we can.'

'They've got him,' she said to Tom. 'He's looking at a long prison sentence.'

LONDON:

AS THE TAXI pulled up to their house, Mary felt relief wash

over her. After all the excitement and drama of the past few weeks, it was good to be home.

Ted paid the driver and helped Mary with their bags, his strong arms lifting them with ease. They made their way up the path, the familiar scent of their garden filling Mary's nostrils and bringing a smile to her face.

As they stepped through the front door, the phone began to ring. Mary dropped her bags in the hallway and rushed to answer it, her heart pounding with sudden anxiety.

'Hello?' she said, her voice trembling slightly.

'Mrs. Brown?' The voice on the other end was deep and official-sounding. 'This is Detective Inspector Harrison from the Metropolitan Police. I'm calling with an update on the case in St. Lucia.'

Mary felt her stomach clench with fear, but she forced herself to take a deep breath. 'Yes, go ahead,' she said, trying to keep her voice steady.

'I'm pleased to inform you that the police officers and gang members who were arrested in connection with your friend's case have been charged and are facing trial,' the inspector said.

Mary let out a breath she hadn't realised she'd been holding, her knees suddenly weak with relief. 'That's wonderful news,' she said, her voice breaking slightly. 'Thank you so much for letting us know.'

The inspector cleared his throat. 'There's more,' he said. 'The authorities in St. Lucia are also working to root out any remaining corruption in their police force. They're determined to ensure that nothing like this ever happens again.'

'That's incredible,' she said. 'Please pass on our thanks to everyone involved.'

As Mary hung up the phone, she felt Ted's arms wrap

around her from behind. 'Everything okay?' he murmured, his breath warm against her ear.

Mary leaned back into his embrace, feeling the tension drain from her body. 'Everything's perfect,' she said softly. 'The bad guys are going to pay for what they did, and Cara and Tom can finally move on with their lives.'

Ted pressed a kiss to Mary's temple, his lips curved in a smile. 'And so can we,' he said. 'Starting right now.'

Just then, the doorbell rang. Ted and Mary exchanged a glance, their eyebrows raised in surprise. 'Were you expecting anyone?' Mary asked.

Ted shook his head. 'No, but I have a feeling I know who it might be.'

He made his way to the front door and opened it, revealing a small group of people standing on their doorstep. Mary's parents were there, their faces wreathed in smiles, and beside them stood Mary's old friend Charlie, her eyes twinkling with mischief.

'Surprise!' they chorused, holding up a large banner that read 'Welcome Home, Mary and Ted!'

Mary rushed forward to hug them, her heart swelling with love. 'What are you all doing here?' she asked, her voice muffled by her mother's shoulder.

'We couldn't let you come home without a proper welcome,' Mary's father said, his voice gruff with emotion. 'Not after everything you've been through.'

Charlie stepped forward, his grin widening. 'Plus, we figured you could use a little celebration after all that drama. I brought champagne!'

Mary laughed, feeling the last of the tension and fear melt away. 'You know me so well,' she said, pulling Charlie in for a hug.

As they made their way into the living room, Mary's

mother and Ted disappeared into the kitchen to prepare some snacks. Charlie and Mary's father settled onto the couch, their voices rising and falling in animated conversation.

Mary perched on the edge of an armchair, her eyes roaming over the familiar surroundings. The photos on the mantelpiece, the worn carpet beneath her feet, the soft glow of the lamps - everything was just as she remembered it.

And yet, somehow, everything had changed. The past week had tested Mary in ways she never could have imagined, had pushed her to her limits and beyond..

Mary thought of Cara, tied to the chair, and now she and Tom were starting their new life together in Birmingham. She thought of Jools, Rachel and Katherine, who had been there for Cara through everything and who had never given up on her, even in her darkest moments. And she thought of Ted, her rock, her anchor, the man who had stood by her side through it all.

As if sensing her thoughts, Ted appeared in the doorway, a tray of drinks in his hands. He made his way over to Mary, his eyes soft with love and understanding.

'Penny for your thoughts?' he murmured, setting the tray down on the coffee table.

Mary reached up to take Ted's hand, her fingers lacing through his. 'I was just thinking about how lucky I am,' she said softly. 'To have you, to have all of these amazing people in my life.'

Ted smiled, his thumb stroking the back of Mary's hand. 'We're the lucky ones,' he said. 'You're the glue that holds us all together, Mary. You're the one who never gives up, who always sees the best in people.'

Mary felt her cheeks flush with pleasure at Ted's words.

Ted leaned down to press a kiss to Mary's lips, his hand cupping her cheek. 'Always and forever.'

As they joined the others in the living room, the champagne flowing and the laughter ringing out, Mary felt a sense of peace settle over her.

As the evening drew to a close and Mary's parents and Charlie said their goodbyes, Ted and Mary stood in the doorway, their arms wrapped around each other. They watched as their guests drove away, their taillights disappearing into the night, and then turned to face each other.

'Welcome home, Mrs,' Ted murmured, his eyes sparkling with love and happiness.

'Welcome home, Mr,' Mary whispered back, her heart full to bursting.

FANCY READING THE NEXT BOOK?

"We'll always have Paris."

OUT ON: 1st of August 2024.

Why not join the Facebook group for news of all the new books: Just type facebook.com/bernicebloom books to join.

ALSO BY BERNICE BLOOM

The Mary Brown Novels:

What's Up, Mary Brown? (The Mary Brown Novels Book 1)

The Adventures of Mary Brown (The Mary Brown Novels Book 2)

Christmas with Mary Brown: (The Mary Brown Novels Book 3)

Mary Brown is leaving town (The Mary Brown Novels Book 4)

Mary Brown in Lockdown (The Mary Brown Novels Book 5)

The Mysterious Invitation (The Mary Brown Novels Book 6)

A friend in need (The Mary Brown Novels Book 7)

Dog Days for Mary Brown (The Mary Brown Novels Book 8)

Don't Mention The Hen Weekend: (The Mary Brown Novels Book 9)

The St. Lucia Mystery (The Mary Brown Novels Book 10)

Fancy reading the next book?
"We'll always have Paris."
OUT ON: 1st of August 2024.

Copyright ©2024 by Bernice Bloom, Gold Medals Media Ltd

All rights reserved.

No part of this publication may be reproduced, distributed, or transmitted in any form or by any means, including photocopying, recording, or other electronic or mechanical methods, without the prior written permission of the publisher, except as permitted by copyright law. For permission requests, contact Bernicenovelist@gmail.com

The story, all names, characters, and incidents portrayed in this production are fictitious. No identification with actual persons (living or deceased), places, buildings, and products is intended or should be inferred.

Printed in Great Britain
by Amazon